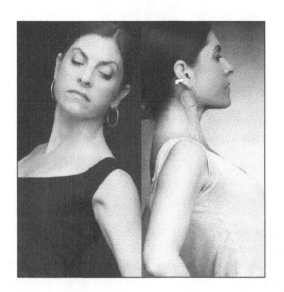

BARBARA BROWNING is the author of *The Correspondence Artist*, a novel. She has a PhD in comparative literature from Yale and teaches in the Department of Performance Studies at the Tisch School of the Arts, NYU. She's also a poet, a dancer, and an amateur ukuleleist.

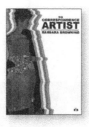

FINALIST FOR A 2012 LAMBDA LITERARY AWARD.

"Browning relentlessly explores her theme of love's many faces, giving readers a rewardingly offbeat novel that's by turns sexy, humorous, and insightful." —PUBLISHERS WEEKLY

"[*The Correspondence Artist*] is a deft look at modern life that's both witty and devastating." —NYLON

"Browning's writing is truly sexy. Playful and evocative, it captures the obsessive nature of love in a way few authors manage. *The Correspondence Artist* is a smartly complex and surprising work of art. More than being simply a 'novel' in the traditional sense it takes that term a step further, existing in form as something truly innovative and new. Part memoir, part fiction, part epistolary, part metadata-existentialist philosophy, part art installation; the sum total is a triumph of a debut." —KGB BAR LIT MAGAZINE

"It's an extended metaphor of a book that nonetheless abounds with insider details, art-world cameos, and precise images – even resorting to the occasional still frame to etch a particular scene onto the mind of the reader." —VOL. 1 BROOKLYN

"Intelligent… a pleasure to read." —BOOKSLUT

"[*The Correspondence Artist*] is wrapped up in powerful feelings of disconnect, confusion, and sexual need. Imagining a failed romance through four different characters [gives] the story an unusual liveliness, and Browning expertly filters critical moments through each imagined lover."
—WASHINGTON CITY PAPER

"Barbara Browning's *The Correspondence Artist* has a conceit that will sound like a dog whistle to readers hungry for a certain kind of high-concept writing. The particular details of these relationships... are sharp, witty, and well-developed: I experienced that nerdy thrill novel reading sometimes gives you when you learn something new... I'm interested in what a Malian musician would have to say to his Lacanian therapist, and the micro-history of ETA we get tickles me the way that getting another strange stamp in your passport might."
—THE COLLAGIST

"Jam-packed with cultural references and lubricated body parts... in a fiction that merges with cultural theory. This is mail worth rifling through."
—THE FANZINE

"*The Correspondence Artist* is an incredibly smart book... Browning both flaunts and expands the form of the novel with this book, one of the true literary breakthroughs of our young century."
—LARGEHEARTEDBOY.COM

"This novel of an affair told prismatically is a love letter to letters, a passionate mixtape to the world of culture."
—THE RUMPUS

I'M TRYING TO REACH YOU

BARBARA BROWNING

TWO DOLLAR RADIO
Books too loud to ignore

TWO DOLLAR RADIO is a family-run outfit founded in 2005 with the mission to reaffirm the cultural and artistic spirit of the publishing industry.

We aim to do this by presenting bold works of literary merit, each book, individually and collectively, providing a sonic progression that we believe to be too loud to ignore.

TWO DOLLAR RADIO
Books too loud to ignore

TwoDollarRadio.com
twodollar@TwoDollarRadio.com

For Viva

All of the moth's videos can be viewed at:
www.youtube.com/AhNethermostFun/

PART I

THE FIRST LINE OF MY NOVEL

I was in Zagreb the day that Michael Jackson died.

When I heard the news, the first thing I thought was, "That's it. That's the first line of my novel. 'I was in Zagreb the day that Michael Jackson died.'" It seemed exactly right – odd, bizarre even, incongruous, an appallingly sad event viewed from an eerie state of helpless remove. It encapsulated all the feelings I'd been wanting to get off my chest, without having any actual story to attach them to.

I'd been toying with the idea of writing fiction – probably as a way of avoiding the real task at hand, which was my academic writing. Given the economic climate and the disconcerting contraction of the university job market, the old saw "publish or perish" was taking on a new urgency. It was making me a little anxious. So sometimes when I sat down at my computer, I'd find myself fantasizing about writing a novel instead.

That first line fell in my lap, but it was entirely true.

I was in Zagreb the day that Michael Jackson died.

I got the news in a text from Sven. "omg did u hear mj died."

All I could answer was, "no way wtf?!"

It was 1 a.m. when I got the text. I went down to the lobby of the Arcotel where I was staying. I was there for an academic conference. It was the 15th annual meeting of PSi, Performance Studies international. The lowercase "international" is not really intended to distance the organization from any Marxist associations. But according to the official website, it's a kind of self-ironizing deflation of any political claims the membership might make for itself. The field of performance studies is definitely left-leaning, but it tends to embrace its own failure. In fact, the conference's theme that year was "Misperformance: Misfiring, Misfitting, Misreading."

Still, while it can be self-deprecating, performance studies claims virtually everything as its object of study – from Indian classical dance and *bel canto* to the "performative" aspects of race, class, and gender. This is referred to as the broad spectrum approach. I locate myself on the more literal and slightly less fashionable end of the spectrum: I study concert dance.

I'd arrived in Zagreb that day, somewhat flustered. There'd been a little confusion with my bag at the airport. For some reason, everybody else from my flight seemed to retrieve their stuff without incident, but after they all filed out, I was still standing there waiting for mine. Just as I was heading to the Croatia Airlines counter to get some help, I spotted it circling around, alone, on an unmarked carousel with the little purple ribbon I'd tied on it for easy identification. It looked like a forlorn dog waiting for its owner. I have no idea how it got on that other carousel. I felt vaguely responsible even though it obviously wasn't my fault.

Anyway, once I got to the hotel and ascertained that all my stuff was indeed in there, I collected myself, washed up, and headed out to check out the conference action. There was an opening reception being held at the Zagreb Youth Theater in the evening. The conference packet said there would be some wine and "traditional Croatian delicacies." Also DJ Chassna would be spinning. Since I didn't really know anything about the restaurants in town and I was trying to economize, I thought I'd call this party "dinner." But when I got to the Zagreb Youth Theater, things looked a little bleak. Apparently quite a few people had opted out of the opening reception and the "turbo-folk" musical performance. There were a few confused-looking graduate students who'd evidently made the same "dinner" plans as me, plus some older members of the faculty of the University of Zagreb Academy of Drama Arts. There were two feuding factions at the Academy – postmodernists vs. social realists. Dan Ferguson, an acquaintance of mine working on a dissertation on the history of the flea circus, whispered this bit of gossip to me as we watched two paunchy, bearded guys tussle over a wine jug. That was apparently it for alcoholic beverages, though there were many cartons of lukewarm "juice drink." Two long folding tables with paper spreads held plastic platters filled with what appeared to be triangular slices of Spam. There was a paper sign taped to the wall saying, in English, "CROATIAN MEAT SPECIALTIES."

DJ Chassna was having some trouble with her sound system. She was pretty, pierced, with a cigarette in her left hand and a cell phone in her right, texting vehemently. Probably trying to get some technical help. She looked pretty pissed off. The soundscape in the lobby of the Zagreb Youth Theater, in any event, mostly consisted of those tussling drama professors, and the shuffling, coughing, and sniffling of graduate students wondering if Spam and lukewarm juice drink were really going to tide them over for the night.

This Spam situation may sound egregious, but it wasn't unthinkable as far as I was concerned. I'd finagled a small research travel grant to get to the conference, but I was living that year on a badly paying post-doc at NYU, with no guarantee of renewal. My dietary choices were often influenced by financial considerations. That evening I made do, politely nibbling at the meat delicacies with a plastic fork, pretending to be hanging around waiting for Chassna to start spinning, even though it was pretty obvious the technical difficulties would be insurmountable. After a while, even those bearded drama professors abandoned their jug of Bull's Blood or whatever it was they were tussling over. I wiped the corners of my mouth with a paper napkin and headed back to the hotel.

Despite my inauspicious entrée to the Zagreb scene, I was trying to appreciate the relative luxuriousness of my situation. The Zagreb Arcotel is a more upscale establishment than I was accustomed to, really – though it had a kind of Eastern European slight offness about it. Or maybe I was projecting. The rooms had hipsterish curtains and throw pillows decorated with black and white caricatures of iconic artists and intellectual figures both historical and contemporary. Richard Strauss, Ludwig Wittgenstein, Virginia Woolf – but also Manu Chao. There was somebody who looked a little like Slavoj Žižek, but it probably wasn't. He was smiling.

There was also a figure that looked a little like Michael Jackson, but on closer inspection it turned out to be Egon Schiele.

I was using my cell phone to take this picture when it started to vibrate with Sven's incoming text. I don't know if I was taking the picture to send to Sven or if I just wanted to remember the moment – but my little exercise in documenting my Eastern European corporate hotel room suddenly paled in comparison. The text really threw me for a loop. I stared at it for a few minutes before sending my generically inarticulate response.

I'd had an uneasy feeling, ever since the luggage incident. But I'd been unprepared for something like this. Because of the time difference I was wide awake – especially after this news flash – and that's why I decided to go down to the lobby of the hotel, where there were a couple of big flat-screen computers set up for guests. I settled into a comfortable chair facing one of them and typed in "michael jackson." A flood of news items appeared. I quickly combed over the most recent ones and ascertained, more or less, the global response to the situation. It was immediately evident the scale of the catastrophe. I glanced up at the several conference-goers chatting on the couches and chairs scattered around the lobby. A few had cocktails. No one seemed to be registering this cataclysmic event.

I went to YouTube. This was, increasingly, my first resort in dealing with questions from the practical to the unfathomable. Of course the platform when it first emerged was a terrific boon to those of us who research live performance, but as you know if you've spent any time on the site, which surely you have, there's all kinds of other useful information people share there. Also not so useful information, and opinions. Sometimes I'd find myself getting absorbed in the weird comments viewers would post on other people's videos. Sven had recently begun ribbing me about the amount of time I was spending on YouTube. He wasn't thoroughly convinced that it was "productive."

My first thought was to watch a couple of Jackson's music videos, but when I typed in his name an avalanche of MJ-wannabes popped up. I started clicking through them. The vast majority had posted their work long before his demise. Instructional moonwalk videos are a genre unto themselves. There were people trying to dance like him all over the world: in Singapore, Sidney, Slippery Rock, São Paulo. A few began or ended with little testimonials. There was a really heartbreaking one posted by a young guy from Belarus. It said, "Small dancing clip for Michael Jackson. I have no possibility to be in the USA. My communication is the Internet. I hope to you will be pleasant this video audition from Michael Jackson." He was a pretty good dancer, and the production values on his video were surprisingly good. Some friends must have helped him shoot it. There was a lot of screen text in Cyrillic, but the official YouTube description was what I just typed, in English. It seemed so sad. He'd obviously invested a lot of hope in the possibility of MJ seeing this video and asking him to perform with him. Even though this had probably always been a long shot, his prospects for such a scenario had now clearly bitten the dust.

I sat there for two hours, from one until three, watching these wannabes. A few were genuinely virtuosic. Some were embarrassing. White people can be so unself-conscious. It's offensive, charming, and pathetic, all at the same time.

One was very weird. At first I couldn't figure out how it found its way into the "michael jackson" related videos playlist. It was called "modéré satie" – and indeed, it was set to Satie's fifth *Gnossienne* – one of my favorites.

A woman in a black leotard, her dark hair pulled back, was dancing a subdued dance in an interior space – her living room? There were some peculiar paintings on the wall. One of them appeared to depict Bruce Lee in *Enter the Dragon*. The dancer wasn't looking at the camera. Her eyes were turned down throughout her little choreography, which was also quite peculiar – not balletic, exactly, though oddly proper. She *demi-pliéed* in plunky time to Satie's moderate little melody, alternately lifting her arms as if to mark the count. Her gestures became more and more idiosyncratic and mysterious, as though she were trying to communicate some information.

Perhaps I should pause to explain that I was at this conference to deliver a paper on semaphore mime in contemporary ballet choreography. I'm a former ballet dancer. I'm learning to say that. Like many male dancers, I started my training relatively late, and ours is not a line of work known for its longevity, so my stage career, such as it was, was pretty brief – and not particularly noteworthy. My longest gig was with the Royal Swedish Ballet in Stockholm. I came in under Nils Ake-Häggbom, and stuck around for as long as it seemed to make sense. I'm trying to transition into teaching, which is why I decided a few years ago to get a doctorate in performance studies, which led to the temporary and somewhat precarious post-doc I've already mentioned.

I was supposed to be revising my dissertation into a book. I had recently been granted a post-doctoral fellowship to support this project. The major revision I'd thus far accomplished was changing the title. The dissertation had been called, *Semaphoric Mime from the Ballet Blanc to William Forsythe: A Derridean Analysis*. By "Derridean," I meant to indicate that even when a dance appeared to be relaying a very clear message, it was always already saying something altogether different. I knew that title might be a bit off-putting to a general audience, so the book was going to be: *I'm Trying to Reach You*. This seemed to have more crossover potential, although the manuscript was probably a little over-specialized for the lay reader, and maybe a tad theoretical. I knew I had to take out some of the extended endnotes, which had nearly the same word count as the actual text, but so far I'd only managed to excise a few commas. I have a slightly pathological attachment to the idea of the "*hors-texte.*"

So, it's not exactly as though I *believe* in singular interpretations, like I could "get" this little Satie choreography if I only had a key. But the dance looked like a message in a bottle. It seemed to have some sort of secret code – the big mystery, of course, being what the hell it had to do with Michael Jackson.

Some of the references were pretty clear: the mudra-like hand gestures ("okay"), which morphed into antlers, and then something like a map of her ovaries; a little Charlie Chaplin walk, ending with a swat at her ankles; a delicate circling of her index finger over her head, as though it were a phonograph needle sounding the clunky little score. And then I saw it: looking down at her feet, she swiveled to the side, and discreetly moonwalked backwards across the floor.

It definitely wasn't virtuosic, but it did have a hint of the uncanny, as the moonwalk inevitably does.

The video ended with her head still down, arms open in a gesture of apparent offering. Then it faded to black. I hit "replay." And then again. Maybe I'd just listened to "Billie Jean" and "Smooth Criminal" one too many times. It's possible I'd lost all my critical faculties. But at that moment, all I wanted to do was hear this moderate little piano solo, and watch this moderate little chamber dance.

The video had been posted by somebody called "falserebelmoth." It had only clocked 6 views, and several of those, as you can see, were mine. I scrolled down to the comments. There was only one, from somebody called "GoFreeVassals": "Kind, icy, slim one… I am raw with lament." That was odd. And yet accurate – as a description of the dancer, and also the response she was producing in me.

I was staring at this comment when I had the disconcerting sense that someone was looking over my shoulder. By this time, all of the other occupants of the hotel lounge seemed to have made their way back to their rooms, alone or in pairs. Aside from a custodial worker vacuuming near the bar, I thought I was alone. I slowly turned to see who was behind me, and to my surprise, it was Jimmy Stewart. Of course it couldn't be, really. Jimmy Stewart was dead. But this guy really looked like him – say, around the *Vertigo* period, or shortly thereafter. He was graying, but still rakish. He didn't even look at me. He was staring fixedly, almost menacingly, at the flat screen of the computer I was using. He pulled some reading glasses out of his pocket and perched them near the end of his nose, leaning over my shoulder to read that weird comment. He was wearing a short-sleeved white dress shirt, neatly tucked into a pair of twill plaid tennis shorts. His white socks were pulled up, and he was carrying what appeared to be a teeny tiny tennis racquet in a case.

I felt a little self-conscious, and also, frankly, put out by Jimmy Stewart's evident disregard for my personal space. I turned back around and clicked the browser closed. When I glanced back over my shoulder again, Jimmy Stewart was gone. I glimpsed him heading out into the Zagreb night with his tiny racquet gripped firmly before him. He carried it like a threat.

I went back up to my room, brushed my teeth, and put on my pajamas. I texted Sven ("xoxoxo"), climbed into the big, flat hotel bed, stared for a minute at the dark, and then went out like a light.

There was something of an international incident the next day. PSi, despite its self-abnegating tendencies, appeared to have provoked some local tensions. It had nothing to do with those feuding drama professors, who were ultimately – even the post-modernists – regular "theater people," not the kind that leaked out into the streets confusing your average Joe about the blurry boundaries between "life" and "art." No, the incident had to do with another set – a group of conceptual artists whose work was being reenacted by an ensemble of actors for the benefit of conference-goers. Their effort, they explained, was not to rewrite the "official" narrative of performance art in Croatia, which, they explained, didn't really even exist: the recent period of political instability and competing state ideologies had only allowed for an unreliable trail of "legends, lies, accusations, clichés, etc." So who knows if any of this is true, but they were ostensibly reenacting the work of people like:

* Sandra Sterle, who, in 2008 supposedly performed *Nausea*, in which she deliberately vomited to the tune of "Dalmatianac nosi lančić oko vrata" ("A Dalmatian Man Wears a Chain around His Neck").

* Siniša Labrović, who in 2007 reputedly performed *Artist Licking the Heels of the Members of the Audience*, drawing attention to a Croatian proverb implying subservience, though this act was held to reposition Labrović in a position of "psychological supremacy."

* Marjian Crtalić, who is said to be, even today, performing a work in progress – 8 years and running – called *Living Dead (Globalization of the Subconscious)*. This piece involves the daily clipping of his hair and scratching of his scalp with his fingernails. "The artist," we are told, "has amassed a multi-year collection of deposits of hair, water and sebaceous fluid from his scalp that is now approximately the size of a tennis ball." According to the organizers of the reenactment, Crtalić has

developed a "paranoid attitude towards his own thoughts and feelings as 'products of a globalized identity "colonization."'" This is further present in the need for purity in the frame of 'my own demented obsessive compulsive boosting of my own deficiencies.'"

None of these recent works, however, seemed to be causing a problem – it was rather the reenactments of two (ostensible) seminal figures from the 1970s that were wreaking havoc in the streets of Zagreb.

* In 1971, Tomislav Gotovac is said to have performed *Streaking*, which perhaps needs no explanation. Ten years later, he reportedly performed *Lying Naked on the Pavement, Kissing the Pavement (Zagreb, I Love You!) – Homage to Howard Hawks' 'Hatari!'* He was basically streaking again, but this time he'd shaved his head and made out with the sidewalk. He was arrested for disturbing the public order.

* Almost exactly twenty years later, Vlasta Delimar, a contemporary of Gotovac who had also been big in the '70s, reputedly performed *Walkthrough as Lady Godiva*, which could, I suppose, itself be construed as a kind of historical reenactment. Anyway, Delimar was also arrested. A lot had happened in Croatia since the '70s, but in the realm of naked performance art, it seems the more things change, the more they stay the same.

So, surprise. The 2009 reenactors of both Gotovac and Delimar, bringing to life a questionable and politically contaminated art history for the benefit of a raggedy assortment of foreign intellectuals housed at the local corporate hotel, were also arrested. I didn't actually see the arrests taking place, but I heard about them as soon as I arrived at the U. of Z. Faculty of Architecture, which was where most of the academic panels were taking place. It made me feel sad and vaguely responsible, but someone pointed out that maybe getting arrested was also a part of the "reperformance." I wondered, though, if they thought they might have been protected by their association with visiting international scholars. But maybe that was just a manifestation of my own projection of a paranoid attitude toward Croatians' thoughts and feelings as "products of a globalized identity 'colonization.'"

Anyway, the incident seemed to get blown over fairly quickly, but it haunted me throughout the day.

I attended a paper on "Peter Sellars: Snake-Oil Salesman or Enfant Terrible?" and another on disruptive audience members. Nobody in our audience was particularly disruptive, though I'm sure a few of us were contemplating the possibility while listening. In the hallway afterwards I ran into Dan Ferguson and a couple of other acquaintances from NYU, and they invited me to lunch, but I just wanted to grab one of the conference box lunches and head back to the hotel to work on my own paper, which I was presenting that afternoon.

It was the same old same old, of course – failures of communication in Forsythe. The ways in which the dancers could appear to be misfiring with each other, but ultimately the dance itself was forcing the viewer to face the absence of meaning.

I know, doesn't sound so upbeat, does it?

I still wanted to tinker with it a little. I gave Dan my cell number, though. He said they'd located the one gay bar in Zagreb and were planning to head over there in the evening. That sounded interesting. I don't mean I was looking for action. It seemed more like research. In fact, I pretty much always feel I'm doing research.

I had to wait a few minutes at the Arcotel for one of those computers to open up. I had my paper on a flash drive. Once I got to work, I spent about twenty minutes moving some of those commas around. I looked at this phrase: "brutal propulsion, contorted mouths, buckling limbs" – backspaced, typed: "brutal propulsion, mouths in contortion, limbs in collapse." Propulsion and contortion sounded too much alike. Tried again: "limbs akimbo." Silly. "Scattered limbs." One step over the line: too violent. "Limbs limning..." – uh oh, my addiction to grammatological figures was popping up again. Maybe I had it right the first time. My gaze wandered, vaguely, to the right of the screen, and slowly the hotel bar came into focus. "Oh shit," I thought. "It's him": Jimmy Stewart, wearing that same manicured tennis outfit from yesterday, or at least a similar one. In the light of day, he was wearing shades – mirrored, with aviator frames. He seemed to be sipping an iced tea. As I stared at him, he slowly turned his head to face me directly. I'm pretty sure he was staring back at me, though with the shades it was hard to tell. He stood there for a minute or so, fixedly, and then gulped down the rest of his tea, tossed a handful of kuna onto the bar, grabbed his tiny racquet, and headed out into the streets of Zagreb.

I looked back at my paper, unnerved. I'd written the first draft two and a half years ago. I'd just managed to move a comma or two, but it clearly wasn't going to be much improved before my panel at 3:00. This reappearance of Jimmy Stewart also wasn't exactly helping my concentration. I saved my changes, closed the document, and ejected my flash drive. I hesitated for a moment, and then opened up the Internet browser, heading straight for YouTube. I typed in "michael jackson moonwalk modéré satie." Up she popped: the tiny dancer. I watched her quietly sink and rise in her mechanical little *demi-pliés*, with her little mudra-hands hanging at odd angles off her wrists. I watched it again. Evidently somebody else had, too: it was up to nineteen hits. I saw from the clock on the corner of the screen that it was really time for me to be heading over to the Faculty of Architecture to test my a.v. before my panel. But I couldn't resist quickly scrolling down to check on the comments. There was a new one, from "quothballetcarper": "Not bad, little lady. Keep practicing." To which falserebelmoth had responded, in a language as peculiar and indecipherable as her choreography: "And I sneered – softly – 'small'!"

I got to my assigned room at 2:50, a little out of breath. I was supposed to be presenting with two other people – the prominent dance theorist Niels van der Waals, and a graduate student from the University of Wisconsin named Amanda Trugget. Amanda was trying to figure out how to open her file on a PC. She was a Mac person. There was a tech guy assigned to the room, but he didn't seem to understand her question. She looked pretty nervous. When I introduced myself she said this was her first conference presentation. She had braces. I helped her figure out how to access her PowerPoint file on Isadora Duncan. Then I checked my own Forsythe images. Quite a few people were gathering around the door, but after chatting and peaking in, they all filed discreetly into the room next door. At about 3:05, someone shut that door, and you could hear the muffled sound of their panel beginning. Amanda and I settled into our seats, and the U. of Z. tech guy politely took a seat at the back of the room. In the awkward silence, Amanda and I flipped through our notes, smiled at each other, and checked our cell phones. I texted Sven: "low turnout wtf?" He texted back: " :("

At about 3:20, I stuck my head out in the hallway, and saw a sign taped to the door. I guess I'd missed it on the way in. It said, "Unfortunate news Professor van der Waals is unable to attend conference." Well, that would explain the quiet migration away from our panel. I explained the situation to Amanda, and she started to cry, softly. I told her I'd be happy to listen to her paper. She pulled herself together, and began reading in a tremulous voice. When she got to the line about how Marinetti had rejected

Duncan's "childish sensuality" in favor of "the 'cakewalk' of the Negroes," she looked up at me with an awkward grimace, her lips stretched painfully over all that orthodontic hardware. I nodded encouragingly, indicating that I understood this wasn't her own word choice. Amanda forged ahead, stoically.

At several points during her presentation, my mind wandered. I was replaying that weird video in my head. I don't think Amanda noticed. I was careful to maintain the appearance of rapt concentration.

When she concluded, the tech guy and I applauded. Then, to reciprocate, I read my paper. Amanda, too, had an expression of polite engagement, but by the end, even I had lost interest. I came up with one lame question for her – the year of publication of the *Manifesto of Futurist Dance* – which she answered (1917). She asked me what I thought the phrase "Fiction (as wish)" meant in Forsythe's *Sleepers Guts*. It appeared as a projection in the background of one of my slides. I started rambling about how, for Derrida, dance has to precede writing... But Amanda's face was clouding over and I let myself trail off. The tech guy was already winding up the cables from the microphones, so Amanda and I just smiled limply and clapped for each other's good manners. We gathered up our belongings in silence and each headed for the gender-appropriate restroom. I don't think it was because we had to pee. I think we both just wanted to get away from one another. It was nothing personal. After washing my hands, and drying them, I stuck my head out into the hall. Seeing no sign of Amanda, I took off for the Arcotel.

Maybe now you will understand why I'd been toying with the idea of writing a novel. It's not that I don't enjoy academic writing, and it's not like I want to be the next Stephen King. Honestly, I love the idea of a paper with an audience of one. Well, two if you count the tech guy. It really had more to do with that question of Amanda's.

That evening someone from the conference organized an impromptu session in the lobby of the Zagreb Youth Theatre where conference attendees could process Michael Jackson's death. Maybe "organized" is the wrong word. I noticed there were not a lot of people of color at this conference. The motley crew that assembled in the lobby of the Zagreb Youth Theatre seemed unsure about whether they were there to speak, or to listen. Someone did, however, read aloud the brief statement issued by the performance artist Reverend Billy (of The Church of Stop Shopping) on his website. It was quite moving. It addressed MJ directly, and encapsulated the extreme beauty and disfigurement of the artist as the logical conclusion of advanced capitalism: "We created you and you created us. I am proud and I am ashamed."

Dan Ferguson texted me that night at about 10:00: "@ gbar mesnicka 36 upper town." I looked up the address on the little map of Zagreb that came with the conference materials. It looked like a doable walk, so I headed out on foot. It was a beautiful evening. Zagreb is a fairly quiet town – not really known for its nightlife. The weather was pleasant, and aside from a few sour-looking elderly pedestrians, most of the people I saw seemed to be teenaged couples making out on benches. They were very workmanlike about this. There was not a lot of laughter or conversation. On my way up into the Upper Town, I stopped in front of St. Mark's Church, which they say dates back to the 13th century. You wouldn't know it – big chunks of it were destroyed and then replaced after various catastrophes, both natural and man-made. The roof has a mosaic of the Dalmatian, Croatian, and Slavonian coats of arms. In the evening light it looked as if it were made of Legos.

I turned the corner and walked up the hill on Mesnička Street. It was very quiet, and apparently mostly residential. When I got to number 36, I wondered if I'd made a mistake – or if Dan had. It looked like a regular row house. But then I saw there was a doorbell with a discreet label saying "gbar." I buzzed, and almost immediately a middle-aged guy with a crew cut opened the door and nodded me in. There was a rainbow-colored neon sign over the bar, and they were playing VH1, relatively quietly. It was dark and air-conditioned. Aside from Dan Ferguson and his three other friends, the only other people in the gbar were the man who let me in, a young, hot guy staring at the video screen, and the bartender, who was a woman. She was also young and good-looking, with spiky hair and a pierced lower lip, but she was very serious. Dan, however, introduced her as though she were already a friend. "Gray, Zlata. Zlata, Gray. Zlata makes a mean Thirsty Lesbian!"

I said, with as much enthusiasm as I could muster, "Oh, really?"

Zlata just stared, waiting for my order.

"Is there something you recommend?"

Zlata said, with nary a hint of a smile, "We have two specialty cocktail, Thirsty Lesbian and Double Penetration. Thirsty Lesbian is wodka. Double Penetration has two kinds alcohol. I recommend beer, Zlatni Medvjed."

I looked at Dan's glass. It had a pink liquid in it that I guessed might be sweet. The TL. I considered asking for more information on the DP, but since I wasn't really in the mood to get hammered, I went with Zlata's recommendation.

Dan introduced me to his friends, who were all, like him, ABD. Sometimes I feel a little old in these situations. I went back to graduate school as what they euphemistically call a "mature" student, but these days a lot of doctoral students are fresh out of their undergraduate institutions. All three of Dan's friends, two guys and a girl, were gossiping about some confrontation that had occurred at the plenary that day. I try to steer clear of academic gossip. I have one of those little figurines of three monkeys next to my computer at home: see no evil, hear no evil, speak no evil. I tried to engage Dan in a separate conversation. We didn't have to apologize for missing each other's paper because we'd been scheduled in the same time slot. I asked him how his had gone.

He said, "Do you want the blow-by-blow?"

I said, "That sounds like one of Zlata's cocktails."

Turns out almost nobody showed up for his panel as well. Then we realized the gbar was also virtually empty. It was a little sad, and a little funny.

Dan and his friends wanted to stay to see if things would pick up after midnight (doubtful). After I finished my beer, I excused myself, awkwardly hugged everybody, walked back to the Arcotel, texted Sven about the names of the cocktails (answer: ":)"), brushed my teeth, and turned in.

The next morning I made the mistake of eating the wall decorations at the Arcotel. It seemed like a good idea at the time. My room, and presumably all the other rooms, had a decorative metallic apple holder on the wall near the desk, stocked with two Red Delicious apples. It was stamped, in English: HAVE A NICE DAY. I'd been looking at these apples for the last two days. I felt one. Definitely real. I figured they had to replace them anyway, so I might as well eat one. I washed it. I took a bite.

It was a shocking mouthful of mealy mush.

This incident made me ponder: my somewhat distressing financial situation; the notion of "decorative" food; the ubiquity of the English language and the global implications of the fall of communism in Eastern Europe; what the maid might think when she found this mealy apple with a humiliating bite taken out of it in the trash can; if I'd been tipping her appropriately in kuna; what it would be like to be a hotel chambermaid in Croatia; biblical representations of paradise and temptation; sexuality and sin. Sven.

I was still hungry, of course. I hoped there still might be some muffins or something over at the conference site. I'd let myself sleep in, feeling my experiences of the day before exonerated me of much responsibility in regards to attending other people's panels. In fact, when I got to the U. of Z., there was some burnt coffee and a bowl of apples in remarkably similar condition to the decorative ones at the Arcotel. Maybe this was just the way they ate apples in Zagreb. Somehow that made me feel better.

I attended a late-morning panel on performance and new media. There was a guy who introduced himself as a "witch doctor" and he compared the manipulation of avatars in cyberspace to the use of voodoo dolls. That was a little disturbing. But then a woman gave a pretty rousing talk in defense of "collective solipsism." She showed photos of an "Air Sex" competition, an installation by Sophie Calle, and an interesting YouTube video of a 12-year-old girl doing the SpongeBob SquarePants dance in her San Antonio bedroom.

This video made me think of falserebelmoth – another small, almost embarrassingly intimate domestic chamber dance.

I really liked that SpongeBob SquarePants dance. But the business about voodoo dolls had left me a little unsettled.

When the panel was over, I grabbed another boxed lunch and headed back to the hotel. I made a bee-line to that computer that I'd started to think of as "mine," and pulled up the performance that I'd also started to have kind of proprietary feelings about. It was up to thirty-three hits. So mine would make thirty-four. This time, though, I couldn't seem to focus on her dance. I was watching her shadow moving across the wall behind her. Sometimes it danced right out of the frame, but then she'd dance it in again. I'm not sure why it would make me so anxious every time her shadow disappeared.

That was when I felt a presence again just over my left shoulder. I knew exactly who it was. I closed the browser just as the dance was ending and sat there with my hand on the mouse, refusing to turn around and acknowledge him. My heart was beating. I'm not sure if I was afraid or angry.

Jimmy Stewart said softly, "Hm," and strode past me and out the big glass doors. The handle of his miniature racquet was jutting out of a small beige backpack. I watched him check his watch, look up and down the avenue, and then flag down the approaching tram. I think he was looking back in my direction as the car carried him away.

On my last afternoon in Zagreb, I decided to skip all panels and meander through the city. The weather had turned slightly overcast. This seemed like an appropriate backdrop to all that Habsburg architecture. I was lamely trying to pick up a word or two of Croatian from the signage in the store windows. It seemed that every 20 yards or so there was a hair salon, and these were marked with the word "FRIZER" or some variation on that term. Like, FRIZERSKI, which was probably the adjectival form. It was odd there was evidently such a preoccupation with hair styling, because despite all that professional attention, most people's hair looked terrible. Croatian people didn't strike me as a particularly unattractive people, but there was definitely a styling problem. Even the more intentional looks seemed badly misguided. It was strange because in many other ways they struck me as quite cosmopolitan.

I took a picture on my phone of one of the posters outside a "FRIZERSKI SALON" and sent it as a text to Sven with the message "the zagreb hair situation."

Then I thought that would be a pretty good name for a band. The Zagreb Hair Situation.

Sven didn't text me back. Maybe he was sleeping.

That night I stayed in, watched a little CNN, and turned out the lights at 10:00 p.m. I had an early flight the next morning. When I got to the airport, however, I found out that my 7:00 a.m. Zagreb-Frankfurt flight on Croatia Airlines had been canceled – no explanation. That meant I'd be missing my Lufthansa FRA-LHR-JFK connections. They gave me a roundtrip taxi voucher, a voucher for a night at the airport Westin Hotel, and vouchers for two meals. They rebooked me for a flight out at the crack of dawn the next day.

The employees of Croatia Airlines were not particularly apologetic. First that weirdness with my bag – now this. I was also a little concerned that Sven hadn't answered my last couple of texts. I sent him another one, explaining, in brief, my situation. I wondered if he'd misplaced his phone. The thought crossed my mind that it might be something worse. But it probably wasn't. I didn't want to add to the drama by sounding worried, so I wrote, somewhat flippantly, "living large: spam on voucher + night @ airport hotel!" I thought I'd start worrying in earnest if I didn't hear from him by the morning.

My taxi driver to the Westin was very nice, in an understated way. In fact, I thought it was possible that he was a little attracted to me. He asked me if I was married, and I said, "No, you?" He said he was divorced with a 16-year-old son. He said his name was Brna, and he gave me his card. He agreed to take me back to the airport the next morning at 5:30. Feeling that Brna, at least, was on my side helped me relax a little.

I momentarily contemplated inviting him up to my room – I mean, not really, I was just kind of joking with myself, but I did consider how funny it would be to turn up in New York with Brna. I imagined Brna eventually meeting Sven. I thought to myself, "If that did happen, we'd probably all get along." I remembered my massage therapist, Ellen, telling me once, "I like Eastern European men. Their depression can be very charming and they're not obsessed with happiness which is linked, I believe, to a more relaxed idea of what breasts need to look like." Ellen is great.

I ate dinner at the buffet at the Zagreb Airport Westin. In truth, the food was not bad. Before I went to sleep I read a little bit from a book on queer theory that enthusiastically quoted the somewhat unfashionable psychologist Silvan Tomkins: "If you like to be looked at and I like to look at you, we may achieve an enjoyable interpersonal relationship. If you like to talk and I like to listen to you talk, this can be mutually rewarding. If you like to feel enclosed within a claustrum and I like to put my arms around you, we can both enjoy a particular kind of embrace. If you like to be supported and I like to hold you in my arms, we can enjoy such an embrace."

Just before I turned out the lights, I got a text from Sven: "sorry. bad day :(better :/ miss you."

I just answered: "xoxo."

Early the next morning, at the crack of dawn, Brna drove me back to the airport in silence. I gave him the last of my vouchers and we thanked each other. The rest of the journey was uneventful.

Harvest Moon

*I*t was good to be back in New York.

I was living in a sublet I'd arranged in those NYU faculty buildings between 3rd Street and Bleecker. Some people referred a little facetiously to these buildings as "The Compound." They were built in the '50s, and they actually look kind of like Soviet bloc architecture. In fact, I kept being reminded of them when I was riding from the airport to downtown Zagreb.

I hadn't been there very long, but it already felt sort of like home. Of course, my capacity to feel "at home" under provisional and precarious circumstances is something I've developed over time. A dancer has to – and in fact, so does an academic. We don't really choose the places we live. We go where the gigs are. After I got my undergrad degree at SUNY Purchase, I bounced around for a while until I landed in Stockholm. I was with the RSB from 1988-2004, which may seem like a long time, but as you can perhaps understand, I always felt a little bit like a visitor.

Nils gave up directorship of the ballet in '93. I worked under Simon, Frank and Petter, and finally Madeleine Onne, who was the one who gently suggested I might want to begin thinking about transitioning to teaching. No hard feelings. I liked Madeleine. I heard she recently took over direction of the Hong Kong Ballet. I wish her well.

Anyway, that was when I moved to Evanston to do my PhD.

At least I was already used to the cold. Sven and I worked it out so that I'd visit Stockholm in July and January, and he'd visit me in April and October. The PhD went by in something of a blur. It was good to get back to reading so much. I like theory. Academia suits me. I actually wrote the dissertation pretty quickly. My advisor said dancers were disciplined. It's true, I'm generally pretty good at setting myself tasks and then following through. It's just the book revisions that have been holding me up. I had no trouble mounting a theoretical argument. But how to make it more accessible to a broader audience? I felt like I'd hit a wall.

Still, I had no business feeling sorry for myself. It was considered something of a coup that I got this post-doc. It wasn't the most auspicious time on the academic job market. There was really nothing in the way of academic jobs in Sweden for the kind of thing I did.

Sven and I kept deferring the conversation about what all of this meant for us.

I was also lucky to get that sublet. It was a studio apartment, but fairly spacious, with a balcony. Nearly everybody in the building was NYU faculty, except for some really old people who were already living in the buildings before NYU bought them in 1964. One of the more ancient denizens of the compound lived on my floor. I'm sure she'd seen a lot of NYU tenants come and go, probably some with little concern for the old timers, so I wouldn't have blamed her for feeling suspicious of recent arrivals. Whenever I saw her I tried to be especially polite. I held the elevator for her as she inched down the hallway with her walker. Sometimes it took her a good three or four minutes. The elevator would start making a honking sound to indicate that I'd been holding it too long, but I persisted. She was hard of hearing so I guess she wasn't particularly bothered by the obnoxious elevator alarm. Once she'd gotten in safely, I'd smile at her and nod. Then she usually said something accusatory, like, "DIDJOO LEAVE DOSE STINKY BOTTLES IN DA GAHBAGE? SOMEBODY LEF' SOME STINKY BOTTLES IN DA GAHBAGE!" She screamed on account of her hearing difficulties. I'd try gently to assure her that I wasn't the culprit, and she'd say, "WHAT?! YA GOTTA SPEAK LOUDAH! MY EAHS AH SHOT!"

After several of these encounters, though, it seemed like she was starting to take a shine to me. At least she started broaching other topics than the accusations. One day we were coming up together in the elevator, and she shouted, "YA KNOW, MY BWUDDA WAS A VEWY IMPAWTAN' POYSON."

I shouted, "EXCUSE ME?"

I thought maybe I'd misunderstood her, but she said it again: "MY BWUDDA WAS A VEWY IMPAWTAN' POYSON."

I shouted, "OH REALLY?"

She said, "YEAH." She paused and looked me straight in the eye. "MEL BLANC."

Perhaps appropriately, I drew a blank. And then it dawned on me: Mel Blanc. The voice of Bugs Bunny, Donald Duck, and Tweety Bird. She was Bugs Bunny's sister.

I said, "WOW. HE *WAS* IMPORTANT."

She said, "YEAH. I KNOW."

After I got back from Zagreb, I did some laundry, went over to the Morton Williams to get some basic provisions, showered, and did a few ballet exercises holding onto a chair for the *barre*. It might have been more productive to take class, but given my financial situation that seemed like an indulgence. That day I did my routine to the Frank Sinatra album *Only the Lonely*, in my underwear: *pliés, relevés, tendus, dégagés, ronds de jambe, battements*. I like to do just the basics, but really slowly. That's why I put on the Sinatra. He's so concentrated.

My sublet faced south, and I guess the people living in the north-facing building on the Bleecker side of the superblock could see me if they really wanted to. I mean, they'd need to use binoculars to see much, but if they were determined, they could probably catch me doing these exercises in my underwear. Of course this made me think of Miss Torso in *Rear Window*, the exhibitionistic ballet dancer across the courtyard. Thelma Ritter's character predicts she'll end up "old, fat, and alcoholic." Hm. Sven and I had watched this movie together when he came to visit in April. Sven was on a film noir kick. We got a few things from Netflix. I hadn't seen *Rear Window* in years, though I read an essay about it in a graduate seminar on feminist spectatorship. It was fairly unsympathetic to the Jimmy Stewart character.

I had a flashback to that Jimmy Stewart look-alike in the Arcotel in Zagreb.

What was it with that guy, and what the hell was he doing in Zagreb? I was pretty sure he wasn't part of the conference – he really didn't seem to fit in with the PSi crowd – but he was definitely passing through.

Well, I had been, too.

After I finished my *barre* exercises, I fixed myself a snack (hummous and raw vegetables) and sat down at the computer to move some more commas around. I did that for about forty-five minutes before I decided to let myself go on the Internet for a minute.

Famous last words. At this point, it won't surprise you that I ended up back on YouTube watching that Satie dance again. I knew as well as you what I was doing, and I knew it meant my "productive" time was over for the day. The moth's video was up to forty-three hits. Who was watching it? I looked at the column of related videos – unsurprisingly, plenty of Satie, a few just piano solos, and a couple of other choreographies, none of which were of particular interest. There was, however, a video of Natalia Makarova dancing *The Dying Swan* to Saint-Saëns.

It was posted by Schoevia. I clicked on it. It's pretty shocking. It's Fokine's choreography, as you may know, but Makarova's interpretation is unique, and people tend to have fairly extreme responses to its convulsive qualities.

The comment section was volatile. BubbleChikk14 started it off: "HER ARMS ARE BEAUTIFUL!"

But arakhachatran responded "No her arms are not beautiful. Thats her worst part in thisperformance. You dont understand anything in ballet but try to act like a smart ass."

That really pissed off yuliya1995 who shot back: "how do you know she has very gentle arms and i bet you cant do that so who do you call a smart ass? its you who is a smart ass who think they know about ballet."

A few others weighed in, mostly outraged at arakhachatran's philistinism. Somebody named ahamayoisac took a more Solomonic attitude, acknowledging that the arm movement was not elegant in a typical balletic way, but was expressive of genuine agony and for this reason "perfect."

Frankly, I love it, but I think arakhachatran had a point. It's practically spastic.

And then I saw it: a recent comment – dated July 27, 2009 – by falserebelmoth. She must have been watching this video, which might explain its popping up as "related" to her own. Of course, superficially, they were utterly unrelated: Makarova's emphatic stabbing of the floor with those pointe shoes, her anguished face and contorted, convulsing torso had nothing to do with falserebelmoth's quiet little moonwalk and her indecipherable downward glance.

And yet.

I'm sure it had something to do with the weird confluence of recent events – the shock of MJ's passing, my dismal, meaningless conference presentation to the singular audience of Amanda Trugget, those disturbing encounters with Jimmy Stewart at the Arcotel… It was difficult not to read some kind of connection between these things, and I felt like the moth was trying to tell me what it was.

Her comment was, true to form, oblique, ambiguous, and strange: "like Birds One Claw upon the Air…"

To which quothballetcarper had immediately responded: "fancy seeing you here little lady. hows the pointe work going? practice makes perfect. i have my eye on you. bye."

She answered, with what appeared to me to be modesty, quiet dignity, and slight defiance: "I cannot dance upon my Toes – No Man instructed me."

He shot back: "Instruction is my specialty, little lady! Ur speakin to the 'pro'! Whippin gals like you into shape is my 'racquet'! Dont think Im goin to go easy on u just because ur a girl!"

Wow. And they thought arakhachatran was obnoxious.

I watched Natalia Makarova dance *The Dying Swan* five more times. Her tremulous, skinny legs stuttered over her pointe shoes. Her mouth was pulled back in a grimace. Everything about her communicated suffering.

"i have my eye on you"? What exactly did he mean by that?

I considered forwarding the YouTube link of Natalia Makarova to Sven but decided against it. Too much tragedy.

The great thing about that Makarova dance is that it's obscene, but everybody acts like it's normal. There are a lot of contemporary choreographers who just go ahead and make the obscenity explicit. People like Marie Chouinard. She'll put her dancers in bondage gear and pasties with prosthetics and toe shoes. I kind of like Marie Chouinard, but Makarova's more interesting to me.

There's a famous essay by the dance theorist Susan Leigh Foster called "The Ballerina's Phallic Pointe." The title basically tells you everything. I could go into detail, but it's probably not necessary. It's a great essay. When I read it in graduate school all kinds of things became clear to me. Susan Foster is smart, and the essay is very erudite, but the tone is a little cheeky. At one point, she says, "*She* is, in a word, the phallus… Now this is a naughty thing to propose." Well, yes, Susan, it is.

I like to imagine what would happen if you passed this essay out to all those stout, pushy moms with their little girls in pink tights at the Joffrey School.

There's another famous essay in the field of dance studies by Joann Kealiinohomoku, called "An Anthropologist Looks at Ballet as a Form of Ethnic Dance." That one also tells you pretty much what you need to know in the title. I often think of that one when people ask me if I do "ethnic dance."

I'd been thinking a lot about Michael Jackson, and not just because of that dying swan. Actually, it was probably hard for anybody to stop thinking about him that week. Standing in line at the register at Morton Williams, I noticed his picture was all over the tabloids. I'm not sure how they rallied all of those editorial forces so quickly. He was even on the cover of *TIME* – just days after his demise. The conspiracy theories were rampant. I usually tend to be a pretty sober person. I'm not particularly quick to suspect foul play. But everyone seemed to agree that that personal physician of his was going to have some explaining to do. And as I said, I had my own personal concerns.

Of course mystery was something MJ seemed to encourage, what with the disguises, the glove, the various things he seemed to be trying to conceal. And maybe it's natural that his propensity for concealment produced in me – as it did in many others – a complicated response. I already mentioned Reverend Billy. Like everybody else, I was a little perplexed by Barack Obama's statement on Jackson's death – but I also understood why he needed to pussyfoot around the issue. You may remember – he called MJ a "spectacular performer" but he felt compelled to add that there were "aspects of his life that were sad and tragic." There were a few different ways to interpret this: as a melancholy reflection on MJ's purportedly abusive upbringing, or as a subtle repudiation of his own purported abuses of others; as a lamentation of his seeming inability to own and inhabit his blackness, or as a suggestion that a racist world had led him to practically flay himself as a sacrificial lamb at the altar of whiteness. I realize my language may appear a little exaggerated. But maybe not so much for somebody like Barack Obama.

On the evening of July 29, the day that I'd gotten home from Zagreb, unpacked, showered, shopped, done my ballet exercises, moved commas, putzed around on YouTube and discovered that uncanny video of Natalia Makarova flapping around like a gorgeous, convulsive fowl, I decided to check in one more time on falserebelmoth. "Decided to check in" may be stating this a bit casually. The truth is, she'd been flapping, moth-like, at the edge of my consciousness, and my own fascination was striking me as a bit creepy. But I couldn't help myself: I went directly to her channel. She'd only joined a month ago, which is when she posted that Satie dance. Five channel views. Two subscribers (GoFreeVassals and that pesky quothballetcarper). There was a short string of channel comments, all from the carper, all in the last few days: "Hi. Two assignments. Learn Harvest Moon. Make a dance in ur bathtub. We dont have alot of time. Practice! Bye." Then, "Back from my vacation at Moms. Aside from my racquet, Ive been using an axe and a chain saw a great deal recently, so when I say that I will hound you until you have produced, you must understand the real threat. I cn be brutal. Dont mistake the mild demeanor." And finally, "Not joking about ur tub. Or the axe. Hurry up, no exuses. And remember, 'Never say sorry its a sign of weekness.'"

The tone of these posts gave me pause. Obviously, he was probably joking – but the persistent axe jokes made me uneasy. I realized the degree of my interest in these private exchanges was inappropriate. It was unlikely that the carper was going to act on his threats. And yet stranger things had happened – like the case of that German Internet cannibal.

Somewhat guiltily, I clicked on the carper's moniker and was transported to his page. He, too, had only signed up a short while ago, and in fact, he only had one channel view – mine being, presumably, the second. He did, however, have a video, evidently just posted. My heart registered with a thunk the identity of the slight, poised figure standing in the tub, eyes downcast, dressed in virginal white: it was the rebel moth! The neck of a miniature guitar, secured by a large, pale hand, was visible in the lower right-hand corner of the screen. The bathroom's fluorescent light cast a dreamlike glow on the frosted glass of the shower enclosure.

The title of the video was "bathtub dance (harvest moon)."
I clicked play.

Another plunky little chord progression started up – not Satie,
but the old Tin Pan Alley tune, "Shine On, Harvest Moon," on
the uke. After four stumbling little bars of an intro, a scratchy,
crooning voice came in:

The night was mighty dark so you could hardly see,
For the moon refused to shine...
Couple sittin' underneath a willow tree,
For love they pined.
The little maid was kinda 'fraid of darkness
So she said, "I guess I'll go..."
Boy began to sigh, looked up at the sky,
And told the moon his little tale of woe...

The "boy" squawked his mild complaint, as the "little maid"
tiptoed her way around her tub *en demi-pointes*. At one point she
executed a demure little bump and grind. The song and the
dance were ridiculous, melancholy, amateurish, luminous, lewd,
indecent, and foreboding, all at the same time. With the last
chord, the scene faded to white, and the ambient echo of the
bathroom seemed to hang for a moment in the air.

I sat there staring at the screen, trying to sort out my feelings.
I recognized that inexplicable proprietary impulse. What was the
moth doing on the carper's YouTube page? Did she want to be
there? And was that him commandeering the uke? She never
looked him in the eye. Then again, she never looked up in that
Satie dance, either. Was she being shy, or furtive, or a little hos-
tile? Was she teasing him with that bump and grind?

His musical performance was equally perplexing. It was something between a lullaby and a howl. Was he serious about this
"boy" and "his gal" business? In the pixelated, low-def video,
it wasn't easy to discern the moth's age, but, to use that term I

recently invoked in reference to myself, she seemed "mature." The carper, or what you could glean of him, looked older still. There was a moment when he leaned slightly in to the video frame, and a small tuft of silvery hair became visible, along with the edge of a pair of reading glasses.

I watched this video three more times, even though I found it somewhat disconcerting. On the surface, it was just another oddball home video, but I couldn't shake that sense of menace. Then I felt embarrassed and told myself I should get back to moving those commas around in my manuscript. I closed the browser. I moved the commas. I stared into space for a while and thought about writing fiction.

That night Sven texted me: "got u a present."

He attached a photo of what appeared to be a cheesy reproduction of Degas's painting, *La classe de danse*, with the figure of the ballet master replaced by a bounding, open-mouthed, alabaster-skinned Michael Jackson. The ballerinas looked on in boredom – one staring at the ceiling, one sucking on her fingers, another examining her slippers – this, in keeping with the original. It doesn't seem like a very likely scenario, really. If MJ were to have shown up in some dance studio like that, I'm pretty sure the ballerinas would have snapped to attention. But the implications were interesting. The painting appeared to be an acknowledgement of his stature as a master of movement.

I thought I knew where this piece came from. Sven works at the Östasiatiska Museet in Stockholm. While the museum mostly houses Asian antiquities and the occasional contemporary art star, there's generally a middle-aged Chinese guy who goes by the name of Andy outside the museum selling his own low-brow oil paintings. These are mostly reproductions of European masterpieces, a few with these oddball substitutions. You can also commission him to feature your face on, say, John Singer Sargent's *Portrait of Madame X*. He usually charges around 750 kronor for a painting, which is roughly a hundred bucks. But since Sven knows him, he probably got a break. Naturally I was very touched that he'd gotten me this present. I'd mentioned to him my preoccupation with MJ ever since receiving his text.

You may get the impression from this gift that Sven has a camp sensibility. On the contrary. He's actually extremely sensitive. That's why I didn't send him that YouTube link of Natalia Makarova. I thought it might make him cry. I'm also not sure how much of a sense of humor Andy has about his paintings. While he gives the impression of being a very happy person, Andy also seems pretty sincere about the things he loves. I'm not really sure about my own degree of irony. I think it's medium.

Sven said he'd put the painting in a tube and sent it by DHL. It would probably arrive in under a week.

It was a little hot in the apartment that evening. I don't really like air conditioning. I thought I'd go down to the garden and sit near the fountain for a while. There's a homely little fountain they sometimes turn on. I took that queer theory book down with me. It was almost dusk, so I knew I wouldn't get much reading done. I'm not sure exactly how I thought I might incorporate this book into my manuscript revisions anyway. It seemed relevant, but if I started addressing more theoretical material, I was pretty sure I'd end up expanding rather than contracting the citations, which were already embarrassingly bloated. I had spoken briefly with an editor from Routledge at PSi, and he asked me about the potential market for my book. I made the mistake of saying something about its "citationality" being of potential interest. I could see from the look on his face that I was badly misconstruing the meaning of *market*.

I sat on a bench in the middle of the garden and opened the book up again to that passage from Silvan Tomkins.

> If you like to be supported and I like to hold you in my arms, we can enjoy such an embrace. If you like to be kissed and I like to kiss you, we may enjoy each other. If you like to be sucked or bitten and I like to suck or bite you, we may enjoy each other. If you like to have your skin rubbed and I like to do this to you, we can enjoy each other. If you enjoy being hugged and I enjoy hugging you, it can be mutually enjoyable. If you enjoy being dominated and I enjoy controlling you, we may enjoy each other...

I'm sure a lot of readers might consider some of this a little comical. It has something to do with that question of irony I was thinking about before. About Sven and Andy and the painting. But I also think that Silvan Tomkins was very sincere. So the business about biting and sucking is really not dirty but sort of sweet and also a little eccentric. And the business about being dominated is really not just about sadomasochistic tendencies. It struck me as simultaneously more tender and more disturbing than that.

It was starting to get dark. I looked up at the moon, which was partially obscured by the branches overhead. I was sitting under a willow tree. There are two very beautiful willow trees in that garden. And suddenly I realized where I'd seen the carper before.

I was sure of it, and it terrified me.

It was Jimmy Stewart. From Zagreb.

THE MAN I LOVE

After considerable internal debate, I decided I was being paranoid. Really, my various "leads" didn't seem to point in any obvious direction except away from my manuscript revisions. I knew I needed to buckle down.

I'm not, as I already said, a particularly paranoid person. I don't generally assume the worst of people.

Sometimes little kids will ask me outright if I'm black. If responsible adults are present they usually look mortified, but I don't mind, of course. It's an honest question. Sometimes very, very old people will also ask me this. This is a little more troubling, as I sometimes get the feeling they might go on to say, "because you don't really look that black," and then expect me to say, "Thank you."

I sort of expected Bugs Bunny's sister to ask me this. But instead, on the morning of June 30, 2009, after making her painstaking trek down the hallway to the impatiently honking elevator as I held the door, after slowly maneuvering her walker into the car, she looked up at me, smacked her gums, and asked: "AH YOU JEWISH?"

I said, "EXCUSE ME?"

She said, "I SAID, AH YOU JEWISH?"

I answered, a little apologetically, "NO, I'M NOT."

She looked at me for a minute, and then she asked, "AH YOU CATOLIC?"

I wasn't sure if it was worse to be totally godless in her eyes, but I find it hard to lie, so I said, "No, actually I was raised without religion. I'm not really a religious person."

She said, "WHAT? I CYAN HEAH YA!"

I said, "NO."

She said, "LEMME TELL YA WHY I'M ASKIN'. I GOTTA FWEN' WHO'S CATOLIC, AND SHE TOL' ME, LISTEN, IF YA EVAH LOSE ANYTING, YA GOTTA PWAY TO SAIN' ANTONY. YA JUS' SAY, 'SAIN' ANTONY, HELP ME FIN' MY STUFF.' LIKE… YA LOSE YA KEYS. YA SAY, 'SAIN' ANTONY, HELP ME FIN' MY KEYS.' AND YA KNOW WHAT?" Bugs Bunny's sister paused for dramatic effect, her eyes twinkling. "YA KNOW WHAT?… IT WOYKS!"

I said, "I'LL REMEMBER THAT."

She said, "I'M TELLIN' YA, IT WOYKS!"

I made a mental note to tell Sven about Saint Anthony.

Bugs Bunny's sister also never asked me if I was gay. I don't really look that gay either.

I'll tell you why I know it was June 30. It's because that was the day that Pina Bausch died.

I was in New York the day that Pina Bausch died.

It was a day I thought a lot about loss, and not being able to find things.

I was out of coffee. I'd forgotten about this little detail when I was at Morton Williams the day before. The weather that morning was threatening. On sunny days, Bugs Bunny's sister liked to take a lawn chair downstairs and sit just outside the entrance to the building in her Miami whites, sunning herself. But since it was overcast, that day she was contenting herself with a chit-chat with the doorman, Jorge. A chit-chat is another euphemism.

She screamed, "HOAHAY, WHAT'S DA WEDDAH GONNA BE LIKE TODAY?"

He said, "Madam, desafortunately ees gonna be more rainy."

She screamed, "WHAT? I CYAN UNNASTAN' YA! SPEAK UP! MY EAHS AH SHOT!"

I dashed over to Morton Williams and picked up some Café Bustelo and a little demerara sugar. When I got back, they were still yelling at each other about the forecast. Jorge paused to nod politely at me and say, "How are you doing, sir?"

Bugs Bunny's sister looked at me and said, "WHAT'S DA WEDDAH GONNA BE LIKE?"

I screamed, "RAIN!"

She screamed, "I TOUGHT SO!"

Back up in my apartment, I boiled a little pot of espresso and flipped through *The New York Times*. I worked on the crossword puzzle. The wind was starting to rattle the windows and the sky looked increasingly ominous. I heard my cell phone buzz against the table: a text from Sven.

"im so sorry pina died :("

I stared at the message. Pina? This didn't seem possible.

I Googled the news and indeed, there it was: Pina Bausch dead, at 68, just five days after a diagnosis of unspecified cancer.

Tears spouted out of my eyes. I felt like a cartoon character. Like my tears were arcing little dotted lines spouting out of my eyes.

Sven knew how sad this would make me. I'd dragged him all the way from Stockholm to Copenhagen on a train a few years before to see *Carnations*. I'd seen it at BAM in 1988, just before I moved to Sweden. I also cried like a baby when Lutz Forster did that sign language interpretation of "The Man I Love." When Sven and I saw it together, we held hands and we both cried. When we left the theater we didn't even talk for a while.

If you've never seen Lutz Forster doing this dance, you should really watch it on YouTube. That's what I did as soon as I'd verified Sven's news. The version that's up is from Chantal Akerman's documentary film, *Un jour Pina a demandé...* First she shows Forster rehearsing the song in a casual shirt. He seems to be in a dressing room. You can faintly hear him moaning the words over the recording of Sophie Tucker singing as he signs with his hands. His hands are so beautiful. The sign for *maybe* is a kind of indecisive wobbling of both hands, palms up. The sign for *home* is an *O* shape that sweeps up from the mouth to the cheek. When Tucker sings "just built for two," Forster holds up two long, thin fingers in the shape of a *V*.

He signs *roam* by tracing a zig-zagging line before him. "Who would, would you?" ends with a wavering gesture, half pointing out, half pulling back.

We didn't have to talk about why this moment was so moving. There's a kind of obvious reading, of course, which is that it makes you think about homosexual desire. Sophie Tucker's voice can say what Forster can only signal mutely. But I don't really think that's the heartbreaking thing about it. If you look at the comments on the YouTube version of the dance, you see somebody called "sagatyba" posted: "nice. made a drunken single_ lady cry. such longing and nostalgia." It's not just for the gays. I think it's more about the *lack* of an object of desire. That song is about the desire for desire, a love object that doesn't exist. Desire that doesn't exist. "Some day he'll come along, the man I love." Some day. But right now, Lutz Forster is wobbling his empty hands, zig-zagging an aimless trail, wavering his extended thumb and his pinky finger before him in some vague question in the conditional. "Who would, would you?"

Of course, you can take all this with a grain of salt. You will remember the original title of my dissertation. My advisor warned me that "Derridean analyses" are really pretty passé. Everybody's moved on to Agamben and Badiou.

That afternoon the sky broke open over Manhattan and the rain came down in heavy sheets. It seemed to me the world was crying for Pina Bausch.

The interesting thing is, Pina choreographed her dancers' tears.

She also choreographed their chewing.

After I pulled myself together, I did my *barre* exercises in my underwear. Then I thought I'd do a quick load of laundry before getting back to moving those commas around. I pulled on some blue hospital scrubs (my housekeeping outfit of choice) and carted my laundry basket down to the basement where they keep the washers and dryers. An older Jamaican woman had occupied the folding table, and she was singing, "Trust and obeyyyyy, for there's no other wayyyyy to be happy in Jesusssss, but trust and obeyyyyy."

She paused to smile at me. She was folding some fancy little toddler clothes. It was evidently not her toddler. I smiled and nodded back.

I was pouring in a capful of soap when Felicia McKenzie came in. Somebody had told me she also lived in this building. She danced for years with Paul Taylor. I think she's married to somebody who teaches at NYU. Anyway, there's no reason she should recognize me, but she also smiled and nodded as she carted her basket over to an empty machine. She was still pretty but a little drawn. Thin. Kind of harried.

I wondered if she knew about Pina.

It was strange, acting as though everything were normal. In fact, I had the sense that my world was under siege. The ominous weather was probably contributing to this impression – but really, first MJ and now Pina… It didn't seem right.

Of course my efforts at revising my manuscript that day were in vain. I took out a block quote from Eric Auerbach, and then realized that the subsequent reference to figures and figuration made no sense, so I pasted the quote back in. I tried switching the order, and then switched it back again. I replaced a semicolon with a period. That seemed like something. Sort of. I popped back down to the laundry room to put my clothes in the dryer. I stopped in the lobby to pick up my mail: *Time Out New York* magazine and some credit card promotions. I prepared myself a light meal (salad, sardines), and afterwards I made a cup of Earl Grey tea. When I finished it, I went back down to get my clothes. I folded them. It was a small load.

I wrote Sven an e-mail about St. Anthony. I told him this tip came from a neighbor but I didn't tell him she was Bugs Bunny's sister. I thought he might find it confusing.

The next day Sven wrote me back saying that it was time to brush up my Swedish for my upcoming visit: the parliament had just enacted the "språklagen" declaring it the "main" language in Sweden. There were more than a few people unnerved by the ubiquity of English.

Sven was teasing me, but I did feel pretty self-conscious about how bad my Swedish was, even after years of living there. So many people spoke English. Sven and I had some little pet phrases we'd exchange, but it seemed so futile to actually try to converse in his language. Sven signed off: "p+k" – *puss och kram*. Kisses and hugs. At least I got that.

Over the next several days, I watched that video of Lutz Forster a few more times. I noticed a clip from Pina's *Água* in the related videos. That was the choreography inspired by Brazil. Frankly, I'm not such a big fan of those choreographies she'd started making in recent years dedicated to particular countries. Even though they avoided the obvious pitfalls of "ethnic dance," there was still a hint of the touristic about them that made me uneasy. When asked about these pieces, she'd always say it was impossible to "capture" a national culture – that she just wanted to present traces of her experiences in these different countries. But the music in *Água* was beautiful – it's hard not to find Brazilian music compelling.

I scrolled down to the comments. A lot of people were looking at Pina's work that week, of course, and posting comments. "RIP Pina! We love you forever!" 85orestes wrote, "Could anyone explain me the meaning of this choreography? You_ see,i'm an ignorant,but this is so powerfull,moving and intense that i want to know more…Please…!" To which Phmerz responded that great art couldn't be reduced to a single sentiment (true).

And then, on July 11, I spotted him. It was that creepy quothballetcarper again! He was commenting on the *Água* video. "Nice, Pina, very elagant, good job! Quick exit to! Need a samba lesson though, hatchatchatcha." The guy was really pissing me off. "Quick exit"? Was that any way to be talking about the catastrophe of her untimely death? And what kind of moment was this to be carping about Pina's samba, as though this were some kind of folklore show? Despite my own mixed feelings about her geographically framed pieces, I hardly thought we should be getting nit-picky about the authenticity of her dancers' footwork.

falserebelmoth, however, had immediately made one of her stinging comebacks: "The Mighty Merchant sneered – Brazil? He twirled a Button…" Hm. That was eccentric. But there *was* a note of hostility, or at least of challenge – now I was sure of it.

I can't deny the small thrill I felt at seeing the moth's rebelliousness. Still, I was also having a vague sense of foreboding.

She hadn't seen that look in his eye in Zagreb. There were those comments he'd made about the axe… And wasn't it a little suspect that he kept on popping up just at the moment a brilliant dancer had died? MJ, the vids, now Pina…

Furthermore, I kept thinking about that tiny tennis racquet. During that visit in April, Sven and I had also watched *Dial M for Murder* and *Strangers on a Train*. What is it with tennis pros and murder?

Joan Acocella had published a piece in *The New Yorker* that week about Christian Comte, a French artist who had constructed animated digital videos out of still photographs of Nijinsky so it looked like he'd uncovered actual film footage from 1912. He posted the clips on YouTube, of course. This was something of a *succès de scandale* in the dance world: a few people seemed buffaloed (*"SUPERBE! MERCI!"* *"tro cool je ne savais pas ke le film existait"*), others outraged ("fake fake fake"), and a third group, which Acocella dubbed "the postmodernists," didn't care if the posted clips were simulacra. They seemed to feel that Nijinsky was a master of fantasy and illusion himself, so why shouldn't that impulse be extended? Comte himself played dumb. That is, his descriptive language seemed to be intentionally vague. When asked, he acknowledged that no film representations of Nijinsky actually existed, and that he'd animated still photographs. But the titles preceding the animations were period-appropriate and artificially aged, as if to add to their apparent authenticity. Also, there was no explanation of Comte's process on his YouTube postings – just brief phrases like, *"Quelques pas de Nijinsky dans 'Petrouchka'"* or *"film Nijinski dans l'après-midi d'un faune."*

Acocella concluded her article: "For many, Nijinsky is not so much a dancer as an icon: of the misunderstood artist, of the mad genius, of the sacrificial homosexual. (He was Diaghilev's lover.) People will take just about anything they can get of him. They want gold, but fool's gold is O.K., too."

I thought of this as I thought about my interpretation of Pina's interpretation of "The Man I Love." Maybe "the post-modernists'" desire for the non-existent, fakey Nijinsky was also the desire for desire. Loving his absence. Loving his impossibility.

So, in the days that followed Pina's passing, I allowed myself a little period of mourning, a brief reprieve from my manu-script revisions to process the loss. I let myself go back and back again to the counterfeit footage of Nijinsky, to Lutz Forster's melancholy signage, and to the two videos of the rebel moth. That first one to Satie's *Gnossienne* was continuing to clock a few hits every day. Obviously mine were among them, and I imagine some random searchers who typed in "michael jackson moon-walk" or just "satie" were landing there. But I also suspected her subscribers of the same kind of periodic viewing I found myself doing. The carper had some pretty obvious stalkerish tendencies. But on July 16, GoFreeVassals left another com-ment: "I am to wait… I am to see to it that I do not lose you."

That was weird. I realized he was articulating what I was feel-ing – which was why I kept returning to the moth's dance. The comment underscored my own sense that she needed protec-tion, but it was also kind of reassuring that GoFreeVassals was on the case.

The painting of MJ in Degas's *La classe de danse* arrived in the mail. I found a big gilt frame at the Salvation Army on 4th and 12th. I framed it myself. I propped it against the wall next to my desk. I didn't want to put a nail in the wall because it was a sublet.

My post-doc was pretty hands-off. I probably shouldn't complain about my penury that year, because honestly, I hardly had any responsibilities. I was supposed to give one public talk in the fall semester at the Department of Performance Studies, and another in the spring. I was invited to attend various other public lectures and performances, but it quickly became apparent that the faculty was happy to leave me to my own devices. Of course I felt honored that André Lepecki had agreed to sponsor me as a "visiting scholar" – I admired his work, and he must have liked something about the chapters I sent him when I was applying for the post-doc. But when I actually showed up at his office hours, I think we both felt a little shy. It's kind of hard to speak casually about things like the choreopolitical effort to transcend the condemnation of the symbolic order by resolutely moving into the quivering ground of being.

There were some awkward pauses.

Still, the connection to the department did give me a semblance of a social life. I was on the list-serve and I'd already established a couple of low-key friendships, like with Dan Ferguson, and Fang Li. Perhaps you've heard of her. She was that controversial Stanford undergrad whose senior art project involved the ostensible use of marmoset stem cells and an elective surgical procedure. They nicknamed her "monkey tail girl" on the Internet. She'd had to field a lot of sexist and racist responses to that one. She was now working on her PhD. She was writing about abjection. Despite her evident willingness to be provocative artistically, personally, she was really sweet. She and Dan and I would sometimes get a coffee together. I never asked her about that tail project. I figured she was tired of talking about it. But we did talk about some new things she was planning, like the intentional cultivation of the world's longest filiform wart on her eyelid. Apparently this was medically possible. We also talked about Dan's flea circus project. They asked me if I was still interested in performing, but I said now I preferred to watch other people dance. Of course I still took class once in a while, when I had the cash. I already told you about my *barre* exercises at home – I did those almost every day.

I guess you could call those "performances" if in fact any of my neighbors were actually watching.

I was preparing for my July trip to Stockholm. I was taking a week (July 20-27), which was our usual. There were a couple of things Sven wanted me to pick up for him: Gold Bond Medicated Powder, Burt's Bees Toothpaste, a couple of little rice paper notebooks they sell at Pearl River. I also sorted out which books I wanted to take: Eve Sedgwick, Brian Massumi, and my dog-eared copy of *A Lover's Discourse*.

My Zagreb trip had just been for four days so I hadn't worried about watering the plants, but this was a little longer, so I needed some help. I gave a set of keys to Fang and asked if she could come by once in the middle of the week.

It had occurred to me to approach Bugs Bunny's sister, since she was just down the hall, but I thought what with the walker, a watering can might be a bit much. She'd begun to ask me for occasional favors. Once she rang the doorbell and asked me if I could read the expiration date on her milk (it was long spoiled). Another time when I came up in the elevator she was standing in the hallway waiting to flag me down. She wanted help calling Access-a-Ride, the NYC transportation service for elderly and disabled people. They make you go through a surprising amount of rigmarole to use this service. Apparently her Access-a-Ride card (like her milk) had expired, and the new one hadn't yet arrived in the mail. Because she's hard of hearing, she was having a hard time understanding the automated messages she was reaching at the Access-a-Ride number. Actually, I couldn't understand them either. The line was full of static and the message kept getting cut off. We tried on her landline, and then my cell phone, which was even worse. When I finally got a real person, I couldn't hear her either.

The bad connection was exacerbated by the fact that Bugs Bunny's sister kept screaming, "WHAT'S SHE SAYIN'? CAN YA JUST TELL HUH I NEED MY NEW CAHD? I GOTTA DOCTAH'S APPOYMENT. CAN YOU HEAH HUH? I CYAN HEAH A TING, MY EAHS AH SHOT! WHAT? YA GOTTA SPEAK LOUDAH!"

Even when I was able to make out what this woman was saying, it didn't make a lot of sense. It seemed like you needed to have some identification number in order to get temporary service before your new card arrived, but the number could only be determined from the new card itself. Meaning basically that this hypothetical temporary waiver was actually impossible. It took several explanations for me to get this into my thick skull.

Finally Bugs Bunny's sister just said, "AW, FUHGET IT, I'LL TAKE A TAXI."

She didn't even seem that upset. This whole pointless telephone negotiation had taken about forty minutes, including the time on hold listening to staticky Muzak. I felt there was something outrageous about old and disabled people being run through this kind of gauntlet for undeliverable social services, but she seemed perfectly happy to throw in the towel.

She said, "MY BWUDDA USE' TA SAY, I GETS IN AHGUMENTS WIT PEOPLE, BUT I DON' LIKE TA HOL' A GWUDGE. YA KNOW WHY? 'CAUSE WHILE YAW BUSY HOL'IN' A GWUDGE, DEAH OUT DEAH DANCIN'."

That's actually true.

Anyway, my point was, I'd asked Fang to water the plants. She was already planning to be on campus so it was no big deal for her to swing by. She's so nice.

The night before my trip, I checked in again on falserebel-moth's YouTube channel. She'd posted another video! It was called "lent satie," and the description just said, "for pina." It was the same background as the first one, with that kooky Bruce Lee painting on the wall, but it was shot in black and white – or actually, maybe in night vision. It had that weird greenish glow of surveillance footage. The moth was dressed in what appeared to be a slightly transparent leotard, and black ballet slippers.

The music was another of Satie's beautiful *Gnossiennes* – *lent*, naturally. As the left hand arpeggiated the introductory chords, she kept her head tipped down, holding a kind of quiet, intro-verted fifth position. But when the right hand of the pianist began to tap out the repetitive single note of the opening phrase, she slowly and demurely swiveled her feet and hips into a synco-pated little trip step: a weirdly abstracted, minimalist, and quickly abandoned gesturing of the samba!

I understood immediately: it was her sly rejoinder to the insensitive and demanding ballet carper! If he wanted a samba lesson, he was going to get one!

As Satie's arpeggios skipped up and down, she marked out corresponding gestures with her mudra-like hands, pointing to her sex, umbilicus, nipples, and eyes. These gestures should have looked dirty – especially with that semi-transparent leotard – but in fact they seemed entirely pure. The only really licentious thing about the whole dance was its most balletic move: when she rose up on *demi-pointe* and waggled there with her hands draped before her eyes, her pubis rocked just slightly back and forth. It was utterly obscene.

I thought of that essay by Susan Foster.

She must have just posted this. Mine was only the second viewing. Of course I watched it again, and again. I was looking for more clues. There were no comments. I'd never left a comment – anywhere on YouTube. I didn't even have a moniker. I just lurked. I'm not sure what I would have said, anyway.

I watched it one more time, and went to bed.

In the morning I had my coffee, read the *Times*, and straightened up. My flight wasn't until the early evening, out of Newark. I did my *barre* exercises, and took a shower. Sven had told me he was going to a "smokefest" at Rålambshovsparken – they were trying to promote legalization of medical marijuana. Sweden is surprisingly behind the times on this issue.

When I'd done pretty much everything I could do to prepare for my trip, I got back on YouTube and looked again at the moth's new dance. Fourteen views, and, no surprise, the carper had almost immediately made his critique: "Nice one, little lady. Need some work on ur turn-out though. Also the colors wierd."

I got in a taxi to Newark. I texted Sven: "*Jag är på väg.*" Well, "*Jag ar pa vag.*" He forgave me the accents. I'm on my way.

DRY YOUR EYES, BABY. IT'S OUT OF CHARACTER.

I took the express train from Arlanda, switched to the T-bana, got out at Mariatorget and walked four blocks to Sven's house. It was sunny out, and still pretty early.

It was a Monday so the museum was closed. Sven was waiting for me. I thought he looked handsome. His hair was longer. We hugged. I whispered into his ear, "*Hur mår du?*"

"*Inte så bra.*" Not so good.

You may think I showed up speaking Swedish because of that new law. It's true that linguistic incompetence often made me feel like an Ugly American, even when I was living in Stockholm, but I didn't really think a little thing like an official proclamation was going to change people's attitudes very much about my language, or theirs. As soon as I got off the plane I was greeted with that familiar old sign welcoming me to "Stockholm – The Capital of Scandinavia." In English.

There were just certain things that Sven and I had a tendency to say to each other in Swedish – the ones we wouldn't really dwell on, like, "I'll be there in five minutes." Or "*Ta mig nu.*" That means, "Take me now." It's a pretty dramatic thing to say in a sexual situation, and Sven understood I was being a little ironic. Still, when I said something like that, it made him smile. :)

We took the day pretty easy. After breakfast and a shower, we had a cuddle. Sven ended up falling asleep. I guess he hadn't slept so well the night before. While he dozed I straightened up the kitchen. I looked over his meds, which he had on the table, along with some materials he'd printed out regarding a clinical trial. He'd gone over these with a highlighter.

He'd told me his doctor thought it would be okay for him to try going FOTO with the Viraday – five days on, two off – to see if it might diminish the side effects (sporadic queasiness, periodic depression, bad dreams). I thought if the doctor thought it was okay, it probably was, but Sven was a little scared.

When he woke up we took a walk. We picked up some takeout at Ming Palace. When we got home we watched *Notorious*.

I'm a little embarrassed to say I'd never seen it before. Neither had Sven. We couldn't believe how good it was. We both loved the Ingrid Bergman character, Alicia Huberman, the ethical slut. There was a moving scene in which Cary Grant defended Alicia's honor to his spy bosses. They were basically willing to throw her to the Nazi wolves in their attempts to secure military secrets because she was so slutty. Actually, Cary Grant had also been psychologically pummeling her for sleeping around, but he finally seemed to have a moment of clarity about the relationship between sex and ethics. He snapped at the big spy boss: "She may be risking her life, but when it comes to being a lady, she doesn't hold a candle to your wife, sir, sitting in Washington playing bridge with three other ladies of great honor and virtue."

Alicia Huberman had so many great lines! Like, "What this party needs is a little gland treatment." We had to pause the DVD and go back to hear that one again. Or, "What a little pal you are." Or, "When do I go to work for Uncle Sam?"

It didn't seem fair that she got all the good lines, because as a Swede she was the one Sven identified with. That would of course make me Cary Grant. When Grant said, "I've always been scared of women. But I get over it," Sven poked me and smiled. It was kind of funny but it was also a little uncomfortable.

The next day Sven had to go back to work. I stayed in and worked a little on my book revisions. That is, I fine-tuned some of the punctuation in the intro, and switched and then switched back again two paragraphs near the end, but then I wanted to check the IMDB for some information on *Notorious*. There were some interesting facts regarding the "MacGuffin" – the uranium stashed in a wine bottle. Apparently that got thrown in at the last minute, because it wasn't really common knowledge at the time that uranium was used to make atomic bombs. Hitchcock was convinced that the FBI was following him around for a while after that.

MacGuffin was a new word for me. Wikipedia said it was coined by a Scottish friend of Hitchcock's, but Hitchcock was the one who popularized it, and exploited it most successfully in his films. It refers to a plot device that hooks the viewer. According to Hitchcock, it came from a story about two guys on a train. One says, "What's that thing up there on the baggage rack?"

The other one answers, "Oh that's a MacGuffin."

"What's a MacGuffin?"

"Oh it's something we use to trap lions in the Scottish Highlands."

"But there are no lions in the Scottish Highlands!"

"Oh then that's not a MacGuffin."

In other words, it's a thing that's of vital importance and central interest, but it may not make any sense, and in fact it may not even exist.

I found that interesting.

After reading the Wikipedia article on the MacGuffin, I felt compelled to return to the rebel moth's YouTube page. I was thinking maybe this MacGuffin business would clarify some things for me.

As you will perhaps recall, the last comment posted before my departure was that mysterious one left by GoFreeVassals. It had apparently flummoxed the carper as much as it had me.

He'd written: "??????"

To which the freedom fighter patiently replied: "You are also asking me questions and I hear you, I answer that I cannot answer, you must find out for yourself."

He could have been talking to me.

Wednesday was a good day. Sven had slept better and he woke up with no nausea. We ate cornflakes for breakfast and played footsies before he left for work. I actually succeeded in cutting out a whole extended endnote on the Vischer-Klamt system of movement notation.

But I couldn't part with Laban. Not that I'm one of those die-hard devotees of his rules for movement analysis. But I just couldn't excise this passage from *Die Welt des Tänzers*: "Like the ecstasies of terror and hatred, the ecstasies of joy and love point to the same contradictory signs. Murmuring and shouting, high and low tonalities combine. Cracked voices, stormy motivations, in which stutters and lofty poetics mix and merge, the motions of surrender and the gestures of pressing-on-the-thing-in-itself [*An-sich-Pressen*] are performed" (179, my translation).

This was another good one: "The solo dance is a duet between the dancer and her surroundings or the dancer and her inner world. In the first case subjectively real, in the second case subjectively ideal" (208).

Guess who that made me think of.

Late in the afternoon I went for a run in Tantolunden Park,

and when I got back to the apartment, Sven had gotten home from work and he wanted to make dinner. He gave me a long kiss and said, "I have a chicken in the icebox and you're eating it."

That's a line from *Notorious*.

On Thursday morning Sven woke up with bad stomach cramps. I don't think it was the chicken. I felt fine. He called in sick and I went with him to Södersjukhuset. I sat in the waiting room while he spoke with his doctor. Södersjukhuset is extremely white. I mean that in terms of the architecture, and the décor. But it was true of the people in the waiting room as well. There was a middle-aged woman who came in with a limp, an elderly guy reading the paper with two pairs of glasses on, and a punk rocker who appeared to have dyed her blond hair black. She had nervous leg syndrome. I nodded at each of them and each one nodded back and said, "*God morgon.*"

When he came out Sven told me that his doctor was not particularly concerned. He'd given Sven an antacid. He thought the side effects would diminish with time. He'd raised the possibility again of experimenting with that FOTO option on the meds. When we got back to the apartment I asked Sven if he wanted to talk it over but he said no, sorry, and he wanted to lie down again for a while. He'd slept badly, with disturbing dreams. He was crying a little.

While he slept I went back on YouTube and did a search. I found a bald Australian guy talking very assertively about his drug regimen. He kept referring to it as a "cure." There was also a travel agent from Minneapolis describing his side effects (quite graphically), which indeed seemed to diminish over time, as Sven's doctor had suggested they might. In fact, the last video he'd posted was really optimistic. He talked for some time about the results of an IQ test he'd just taken. Apparently not only was his viral load undetectable – he was also smarter than he'd suspected. He didn't give the precise figure, but he said, "It was kind of a surprise, because with the anxiety, sometimes I feel like maybe I'm not so intelligent, but when I got the results of the test, well, let's just say I was pleasantly surprised."

There was a slew of recent videos posted by a 24-year-old guy in San Antonio, Texas, talking about how he was handling the side effects of Atripla (brand name version of Sven's Indian knock-off meds). He'd just recently been diagnosed. He also had anxiety and a stomachache, but he tried to remain upbeat.

This research was simultaneously reassuring and a little demoralizing. What else could I watch? The SpongeBob SquarePants dance? Something with cats? I ended up on falserebelmoth's channel page. She'd put up a new video!

It was called "ipod samba." The description read: "Breath – and I." I clicked on it.

She was back in that same odd little domestic setting, though now evidently in the daylight. She was wearing vaguely athletic clothes, and had on Converse sneakers, which slapped the floor as she danced. In fact, this slapping of her feet against the floor constituted the entire soundtrack of the video, though she herself appeared to be listening to something on the titular iPod hanging around her neck.

Her eyes were closed, but she was smiling a little, with an expression of what you might call sensual abandon. I wondered if she were a little drunk. The slapping of her shoes created its own percussive pattern, broken sporadically by a pause, a moment's hesitation, a hovering over the beat. And then she'd gamely grind her hips, and shuffle in a circle, that half-smile on her lips. The video was two minutes and twenty-four seconds long. At about 0:34, you began to hear her breathing. Her in- and exhalations were in time with the patter of her shoes. The sound of her lungs increased in volume and intensity until, at the very end, it was a positive cacophony of lungs and slapping feet, and then suddenly she popped back on her heels, opened her mouth in a broad smile, inhaled deeply, wiped the sweat off her brow, and abruptly walked out of the frame.

She seemed to be enjoying herself so much. Eyes closed, earbuds in her ears.

I watched it four more times.

That evening Sven didn't feel much like having dinner, but I heated up some soup and brought it to him in bed, with knäckebröd. He had a little. He also didn't feel like reading, or watching a movie. He apologized and I told him not to be silly.

At about 11:00 I brought him his meds and a glass of water. Viraday comes as one huge, salmon-colored tablet. It's a little hard to swallow, but Sven didn't bother breaking it in half. He looked at it in the palm of his hand before he put it in his mouth and washed it down with a mouthful of water. He grimaced and lay back on his pillow.

I smoothed the hair away from his eyes, and he reached up and touched my cheek. I remembered Cary Grant and the way he looked at Ingrid Bergman when he discovered that Claude Rains and his mother had been slowly killing her with poison.

:(

The next morning Sven felt pretty good. He even wanted to eat Kalles on his knäckebröd. Kalles is a kind of creamed cod roe sold in what resembles a toothpaste tube – it's pretty gross. He took a shower and kissed me on the lips before he left for work, and it seemed like everything was just fine.

I put Sinatra on and did my *barre* exercises in Sven's living room. Then I sat down with the Eve Sedgwick book. This was the one with those long citations from Silvan Tomkins. Tomkins said that even two "sociophilic," i.e. perfectly nice, people could sometimes experience difficulties in their relations:

> … you may crave much body contact and silent communion and I wish to talk. You wish to stare deeply into my eyes, but I achieve intimacy only in the dark in sexual embrace. You wish to be fed and cared for, and I wish to exhibit myself and be looked at. You wish to be hugged and to have your skin rubbed, and I wish to reveal myself only by discussing my philosophy of life.

That was kind of sad. I refrained, however, from incorporating this into my academic manuscript. I thought, "Maybe if I write that novel…"

After a couple of hours of thwarted efforts at productivity, I caved in and went to falserebelmoth's channel page. My excitement about her having posted a new dance was counterbalanced by some mild anxiety about the comments it might have elicited. It was up to eleven hits. And – no surprise – both the carper and the liberator had weighed in.

quothballetcarper declared: "Pretty good little lady! I can almost feel the breaze blowing in over Copacabana! Hatchathatcha! Hey, R U DRUNK???"

To which she answered: "Do we 'get drunk'? Ask the jolly clovers!" This appeared to be some kind of special moth reference, tinged with her distinctive insouciance.

GoFreeVassals practically swooned: "Your breath falls around me like dew – your pulse lulls the tympans of my ears"

And she responded: "a Drum – Kept beating – "

I couldn't help but notice there seemed to be some sort of sexual tension between the moth and the liberationist. This exchange was what you might call throbbing. Not threatening – but strangely intimate. I felt embarrassed to be looking in.

That night after a cuddle Sven had a panic attack. It was kind of frightening for me as well. He turned his back to me and hugged his knees to his chest. He was making very small wheezing sounds. I stroked his hair. It was so silky and golden between my fingers. I looked at the down on the back of his neck. I nestled up against his back and held him. I said softly, "*Andas ut*." Breathe out.

It took a long time for us to fall asleep.

Saturday Sven texted me from work saying, "iran protest sergols torg wanna go?" You may remember – this was shortly after the clampdown on Iranian protesters, and there were sympathetic manifestations all over the world. I'd been following the news every day, but in a slightly distracted way, what with my more immediate concerns about Sven.

Still, I thought it was a pretty significant issue, and I was also curious about how the eminently civil Swedes would express themselves. And I found it encouraging that Sven seemed to care enough to want to go. On a lighter note, he told me that that "smokefest" for the legalization of cannabis had yielded about twenty-five hippies. He showed me the news coverage on YouTube. One of the spokespeople was a blond guy with dreadlocks stuffed into a knitted cap who sounded really reasonable and not at all stoned. Sven also pointed out a friend of his who was reclining with his arms over his head. He said his name was Filip. He gave Sven a joint. Joint in Swedish is "joint."

Anyway, we agreed to meet later in the day at Sergols torg. The protest was much bigger than I'd anticipated. There were about a thousand people. The center-right politician Birgitta Ohlsson spoke. Her brand of neo-liberalism is not exactly my taste, nor Sven's, but these kinds of situations sometimes make for strange political bedfellows. There were lots of Iranian flags, and some Swedish ones. There were signs in Persian, and Swedish, and English. Lots of people had big photographs of Neda Agha-Soltan, the young woman who had been killed.

Sven stared at a poster with her face on it. He said, "She was so pretty. She was so young." I thought he was going to cry.

That night we wanted to watch the news about the protest. There had been similar ones all over the world. Apparently the one in Stockholm had been among the largest. But the lead story was, in fact, something entirely different: a fire that had broken out in Rinkeby. A forty-two-year-old Somalian woman and her five daughters, aged one to sixteen, had been killed. It was the deadliest fire in Scandinavia in many years. The woman and her kids were apparently trapped in the elevator, and asphyxiated.

It was terrible. Sven and I watched the report and didn't say anything.

Rinkeby is a suburb just west of Stockholm. It's got a very large immigrant population. In fact, some people call a certain kind of immigrant dialect "Rinkebysvenska." I realize dialect is a troublesome word. Swedes are pretty attentive to the politics of multiculturalism. It is more properly called a "multiethnolect" because it mixes Turkish, Arabic, Serbian, English, and Spanish. Some people call it "Shobresvenska" which is something like "Hey Bro Swedish," the "hey bro" part, *sho bre,* coming from the Arabic.

There had been a lot of immigrants at the protest that day. One young guy had nodded at me and said, "*Sho bre.*"

We were so disturbed by the story about the fire neither of us felt like making love. We went to sleep just lying next to each other. Surprisingly, Sven slept pretty deeply that night, and he was able to eat all right in the morning. We were still melancholy. Even though there was something heartening about seeing everybody come out for the protest in Sergels torg, nobody was sure if it was going to come to anything. I'd felt strange clapping for Birgitta Ohlsson. The news coming out of Iran was still not good. I had my own misgivings about turning Neda Agha-Soltan into some kind of poster girl for the green revolution, but it's true that it was difficult to keep looking at her face on those posters. And then there was the tragic story of that Somalian woman and her daughters.

We tried to put a good face on things for my last full day in Stockholm, but neither of us was very good at faking it.

And to cap it all off, the next day, while I was riding the train back to the airport, reading *A Lover's Discourse*, my cell phone began to vibrate. Sven was texting me the news.

Merce Cunningham was dead.

I stared at my phone and a tear rolled down my cheek.

As Cary Grant so eloquently put it: I was a fatheaded guy, full of pain.

A RIGOROUS SADNESS

*O*mg merce är död :("
    I was in Stockholm the day that Merce Cunningham died.

He was all I could think about on the flight home.

I'd taken some classes at the Cunningham studio – first years ago, with Merce himself, before my time in Sweden, and then a few times just for diversion since I'd been living in the Village. It was walking distance, and I liked to go over there sometimes on Saturdays, when it wasn't just the competitive young dancers. The classes were taught by a company member. On the weekend, all kinds of kooks and old-timers would show up.

Sometimes you'd still see Merce himself getting pushed around in his wheelchair by one of his handsome, young assistants. He'd look right at you and smile. He had that whispy white halo of hair, and those impish eyebrows.

I'd taken Sven to see his company in Chicago, back when I was in graduate school. It was in October of 2007, and Sven was visiting that week. They performed *eyeSpace*, the piece in which audience members were all listening to iPods, so everybody had a different soundscape for the dance. They also performed an early piece, *Crises*. Originally Merce had danced it, with four women. When we saw it, Rashaun Mitchell danced Merce's part. It's funny, I typed "Merce's role" and then changed it to "part" because with Merce you don't generally think about theatrical personae. Things are so abstract. He was pretty explicit about that. But even he said that *Crises* was "dramatic," despite the fact that it was non-narrative. You almost can't help construing something about what this man feels toward these four women. The score to that one was for a player piano. It's mildly comical, though disconcerting.

Now I just had a flashback to that uncomfortable little poke in the ribs Sven gave me about that line, "I've always been afraid of women." Sven didn't really mean women, of course. He just meant intimacy.

I took a taxi from Newark. I thought about taking the Path train but it seemed like too much of a hassle. Halfway home I got into a mild panic about how much ground transportation cost. It was nearly the end of the month, which was generally when my bank balance was hovering just above zero.

I got back to the apartment and dumped my bag on the couch. I took a quick shower, put on my underwear, and did some stretches to Abbey Lincoln with my eyes closed. When I was done I checked on the plants. Not only had Fang watered them – she'd also left a couple of small plastic deer embedded in the dirt. They seemed a little afraid, but only if you looked them in the eye. I guess that's why they have that expression, "like a deer caught in the headlights." Anyway, I thought this was very thoughtful of Fang.

Then I made myself some mint tea and sat down at the computer. It won't surprise you to learn that the first thing I did was to look up Merce's obituary in the *Times*. It was by Alastair Macaulay. For him, it was surprisingly tender (Macaulay can be pretty acerbic). He talked about what a remarkable dancer Merce had been, and he talked about his domestic relationship with John Cage, which had been an "open secret" for so many years. You usually hear people refer to Merce as the more serious one, and Cage as providing the comic relief. But Macaulay hinted that maybe Cage had been a bit "controlling" at home. He quoted Merce after Cage's death in 1992: "On the one hand, I come home at the end of the day, and John's not there. On the other hand, I come home and John's not there."

I actually found this very poignant, and it made me feel a little better about Merce's passing. He seemed pretty Zen about death. When I read that quote, it seemed to me it was as though Cage had gone on vacation and Merce was getting a little break.

Of course Cage himself was pretty Zen. To say the least. The Walker Art Center had just posted an interview on YouTube with both Cage and Cunningham from 1981. They didn't identify the woman asking the questions; it seems funny to even call her a woman – she looked so young. She gave you the impression that she was wearing braces, even though she wasn't. In fact, she reminded me of Amanda Trugget. She seemed very bright – just young. She was interviewing them in a dance studio, and you could hear somebody in the background rustling some materials around.

True to form, Cunningham was the more staid one, and Cage kept giggling. If he weren't sixty-nine, you might have assumed he was stoned. Well, I suppose he could have been. Anyway, there was this funny moment when Cage was talking about how people had become more accepting of their artistic shenanigans over the years, and he thought maybe it was because they were getting old: "Now that we're more or less on our last legs the audience is beginning to sit up and enjoy itself."

The phrase "last legs" seemed to make the young woman a little uncomfortable. She murmured nervously, "That's great…"

Cage giggled and said, "Well, maybe it'll continue for a little while…"

She mumbled, "Uh… hope so…"

He also said something about how critics started wondering when Merce would quit performing when he hit forty, but now that he was *really* old, people couldn't get enough of him.

It was hard to tell what Merce was thinking while Cage was talking. He looked like he might have been vaguely irritated. But I could have been projecting.

Cage died eleven years after that interview, but Merce lasted another twenty-eight.

Speaking of very old people: when I went out to pick up some groceries early that evening, I saw the maintenance man coming out of Bugs Bunny's sister's apartment. He had on a tool belt and he was standing there in the hallway as she screamed at him from just inside her apartment.

"SO IT'S WOYKIN' NOW?"

"Ees okay, ees juss a leel... you juss gonna pay tainshun wenna you flushing. You juss gonna hola downa da hendel..."

"WHAT? YA GOTTA SPEAK LOUDAH, MY EAHS AH SHOT!"

The maintenance guy looked at me, it seemed, imploringly. I stuck my head in her doorway and shouted, "HOLD THE HANDLE DOWN WHEN YOU FLUSH!"

She nodded: "OKAY GOT IT." She smacked her gums, and then smiled and gave us both a thumbs-up.

As we walked toward the elevator, she stuck her head out the door and shouted, "WAS DAT YA GOYLFWEN'? DAT CHINESE GOYL? I SAW A CHINESE GOYL GOIN' IN YA APAHTMENT."

I said, "JUST A FRIEND."

She said, "CUTE. VEWY CUTE."

We smiled at each other and she gave me another thumbs-up.

It was true, Fang was cute. But weird. I guess Bugs Bunny's sister didn't notice that part. Fang made a lot of her own clothes, or modified things she picked up at the Salvation Army. She did that free-form style of crochet that resembles seaweed, or fungus. I think they call it "scrumbling." She would attach pieces of this to the necklines of her shirts, and the tops of her boots. Sometimes she used fibrous organic materials like shredded banana peels or leaves that would start to smell a little funny after a while.

She had a bracelet she'd made out of hardened goose shit that she found near Prospect Park.

She also had a pierced septum. Every time I looked at it I thought of that Edward Lear poem, "The Owl and the Pussycat," in which the unlikely newlyweds have to travel very far in a boat in order to find a ring, and they get it from a pig who's wearing it in his nose.

So I guess Bugs Bunny's sister just saw Fang from a distance, because I think if she'd gotten a good look at the septum ring or the scrumbling, she might have found it a little off-putting. If you didn't get too close, Fang looked pretty normal.

I texted Fang that night to invite her out for a beer, in order to thank her for taking care of the plants. As I said, I was pretty low on cash money, but I was expecting a direct deposit of my fellowship payment in two days and thought I'd probably make it until then, even treating Fang. I texted Dan Ferguson, too. He suggested we meet at Marie's Crisis, which is a supergay piano bar in the West Village where the patrons all sing show tunes. Fang and I didn't know most of the words to the songs (except for the really obvious ones like "My Favorite Things"), and even Dan isn't really a belter, but it was fun. I started to tell them the story about Merce and what he said when Cage died, but I gave up halfway through because it was really loud and they couldn't hear me. Still, it cheered me up a little, going out.

Over the next few days, I watched a lot of Merce. There were some more interviews, and films of him giving class in his studio. These reminded me of the few classes I'd had with him years ago. He was very understated. The phrase he used most often was, "Okay, go."

I watched him in some old archival footage dancing in Martha Graham's *Appalachian Spring*. I watched the Charles Atlas films, and *Beach Birds for Camera*. But the film that I found most beautiful was an excerpt from *Septet*, which he composed in 1957, although the film was of a performance in 1964. The excerpt is of the section danced to the *En Plus* movement. Even though he was already collaborating with Cage, *Septet* was set to Satie –*Trois morceaux en forme de poire*. I'm not sure why Satie called it three pieces, since there are seven parts, and it's difficult to say what's pear-shaped about them. They were piano pieces to be played by four hands.

En Plus is the most beautiful. Merce dances this section with three women. One of them is Carolyn Brown (exquisite). I'm not sure who the other two were. The choreography is very slow and controlled. Merce tends to occupy the center, and at times the three women appear to be allegorical figures (muses?) framing him. They lean into each other, or away, finding a kind of off kilter balance. The orientation keeps shifting, and you're often aware of geometry, torque, and perspective, and yet there are moments when they'll assume a pose and you're tempted to read some kind of emotionalism into it. At one point all three women are arranged slightly askew of Merce, but they kind of tilt their heads and look at him. He's on one knee with his left leg extended before him, and he seems to bow his head down to Carolyn Brown, maybe sadly, maybe respectfully.

Just a couple of years ago Carolyn Brown published a memoir of her years with Merce. She said it wasn't always easy. She loved him but he could be a little chilly. But at the end, when it was time for her to stop dancing, she said he treated her with "exceptional kindness." After her last performance, after she took her bows, she went to his dressing room. She wanted to thank him. He said, "It's been a wonderful twenty years. You're beautiful and I've never told you enough."

People often know when they don't say enough.

Sven of course was concerned about how I was taking Merce's death. I sent him the links to a couple of the YouTube videos — *Septet*, and that interview with Cage. When I suggested Cage might be stoned, he responded ":)," which was funny because that's exactly what Cage looked like when he giggled.

I asked him how things were going with his meds and he said a little better. *En lite bättre.*

I ran into Bugs Bunny's sister that week in the hallway. She had just come back from Morton Williams and she was having a difficult time negotiating the key to her place, the walker, and her groceries, so I offered to help her. She seemed genuinely appreciative. She said, "YAW A NICE YOUNG MAN. I WASN'T SO SHUAH WHEN I FOYST SAW YA, BUT YAW A NICE POYSON." She winked at me when she said this, as though she were joking about her early suspicions, but it was probably true. As I said before, I couldn't blame her.

I asked her if she needed any help putting things away. She said, "NAH, BUT COME ON IN FAW A SECON'. I WANNA SHOW YA SUMP'N."

Her apartment had a lot of stuff in it. I guess that's not surprising since she'd been living there for about 50 years. There were lots of tchotchkes, and quite a few shopping bags of stuff on top of the chairs and tables. I was wondering where it was she sat down.

She said, "WAIT A MINUTE, I WANNA SHOW YA SUMP'N. I FOUN' IT TODAY, I CYAN' BELIEVE I STILL GOT IT."

She wheeled her walker into the kitchen, rummaged around for a while, and came back with something small gripped between her fingers as she simultaneously clung to the handle bars of the walker. She slowly made her way toward me and then held it out for me to examine: a matchbook with a garish, color-ful illustration. She didn't have to tell me what it was, but she did.

"IT'S SIEGFWIED AND WOY! I SAW 'EM AT THE STAHDUST IN 1978. DAT WAS A GWEAT SHOW. DEY WAS TWO GOOD-LOOKIN' GUYS, I'M TELLIN' YA! LOOK!"

I said, "WOW, THAT'S GREAT." I hesitated, but then I asked, knowing how much Sven would love this. "CAN I TAKE A PICTURE OF THIS WITH MY CELL PHONE?"

She looked perplexed, and said, "WHAT?"

I repeated the question, showing her my phone. Evidently the problem wasn't that she thought it was a weird thing to want to photograph. She just wasn't that familiar with this particular use of a phone. But when she got what I was suggesting, she said, "OH SHUAH, TAKE A PICSHA!"

I did.

Later that day I texted Sven, and attached the photo. I thought about making a joke about them looking kind of like us, but then I didn't. Sven seemed more interested in the tiger between them. He said, "nice tiger."

I was trying to draft a letter to the academic presses to which I planned to submit my manuscript. Wesleyan seemed like an obvious choice. I also wanted to approach Routledge (despite the little faux-pas I'd made about my book's "market" at PSi), and possibly Illinois, which seemed to be expanding its dance publications, despite the general contractions of university presses. For the narrative overview of the project, I began by cutting and pasting from my dissertation's abstract, but I was pretty sure the editors' interest would begin to flag around the third sentence, when I began dog-paddling into the murky waters of "grammatological impossibility." I pulled up the Microsoft Word Reference Tools to see if I could find a better phrase. The thesaurus didn't contain "grammatological" but suggested I might mean "grain elevator, grain sorghum, grain weevil, grained, or grains of paradise." The best replacement for "impossibility" seemed to be "ridiculousness." I wondered if I should be trying to make this book sound more like a comedy.

Just a couple of weeks before Merce's death, there'd been a story in the *Times* about the "legacy plan" he was developing with his company. He knew he wasn't going to be around forever, and wanted to make a plan for preserving his work. Actually, *preserving* isn't the word – he was determined not to mummify it, but to allow it to move gracefully into the world and assume different configurations in its afterlife. At the same time, he wanted to make sure his company members would be able to transition into the next stage of their careers, without him. He wanted for the company to continue touring with the repertory for a period of two years, and then to disband. He wanted to set aside funds for the company members to have a year's salary as severance pay, along with "extra money to help find new careers." Staff members and musicians would also be looked after. Merce's Trust would oversee licensing of his choreographies, and his former dancers and archivists would establish "dance capsules" – digital pods containing video documentation, lighting plans, décor and costume designs, production notes and so on. These could be accessed by researchers, or by dancers interested in recreating the pieces. But Merce knew that any future forms the dances would take would be, of necessity, different.

He told the reporter for the *Times*: "It's really a concern about how do you preserve the elements of an art which is really evanescent, which is really like water... It can disappear. This is a way of keeping it – at least with our experience here – of keeping it alive."

I'd read this article when it came out, which was just shortly after Pina's death. So I'd read it thinking of Pina. Now I went online to read it again. When I was searching for it, I found another version of the same story published at about the same time in *The Wall Street Journal*. It was by Terry Teachout. It was titled: "Why Dances Disappear: Can Merce Cunningham Save His Work by Killing His Company?" Obviously, the headline was supposed to grab your attention – Merce didn't really want to "kill" his dancers – and in fact Teachout's depiction of Merce was very affecting: "instead of trying to keep his company alive in order to preserve his dances 'as is,' he's going to send them out into the world and let them make their own way. That sounds very much like the decision of a wise parent, one who loves his children, trusts them to do the right thing – and knows that, sooner or later, they'll have to fend for themselves."

It's interesting, though – I had to read that paragraph several times to figure out whether Teachout was talking about his wishes for his dancers or for his dances. Actually, I'm still not sure.

The tongue-in-cheek sensationalism of the title of that article, implying that Merce had murderous tendencies, did manage to set off my mild but increasing paranoia – not that I was actually suspecting Merce of any wrongdoing. On the contrary, I felt it was *his* demise that was looking a little suspicious. I mean, rationally, I knew he was very, very old, and he'd been working out these "legacy" plans precisely because everyone knew he didn't have much time. But it was so *weird* that his death occurred so quickly after MJ's, and then Pina's. I'm sure you're shaking your head as you read this. There was a logical explanation for everything. But it didn't help matters that all too soon I discovered that dubious ballet carper lurking around the scene of the crime.

In the midst of my week of YouTube Merce immersion, I paused to check in on the rebel moth. It was partly the discovery of Merce's Satie choreography, which made me think of hers – but also, I was just missing her. To my delight, she'd posted a new dance! It was set to Satie's final *Gnossienne*, *Avec conviction et avec une tristesse rigoureuse*. The description said, merely: "It might be lonelier / Without the Loneliness – " It was clear to me that she was memorializing Cunningham. And Cage.

It was her first partnered dance. That is, *partnering* is a funny term to use to describe this piece.

Partner is actually a word that irks me. I mean in virtually all the contexts in which it's used. Sven rolls his eyes when I say this. But this is what I mean: obviously there's an overdetermined history to the idea of partnering in Western dance – especially ballet. I already told you about that essay by Susan Foster, about the "ballerina's phallic pointe." You get the idea: the male dancer holds the ballerina in front of him and she sticks out her long pink leg with its stiff pink prosthetic extension protruding off the end of her foot. He wags her around at the audience as if to say, "Look at this long pink stiff thing I am wielding around before you."

Of course there's plenty of classical, romantic choreography that I enjoyed dancing, and I can see the beauty, but let's face it, there are problems with this.

Modern dance changed a lot of that, and maybe Merce was the most interesting one to play with classical ideas about partnering, but it's almost because he maintained some of the premises of ballet that he made it interesting. There were other people, contact improvisers, wacky postmodernists, interculturalists, who did some pretty radical things. But Merce changed the relation even though he often worked with male/female pairings. In *Septet*, right after that moment when he bows his head down to Carolyn Brown, he rises, moves behind her, and holds her as she slowly dips down in a deep *attitude devant* in *grand plié*. He seems to be supporting her tenderly. But what holds them together is difficult to pin down.

In her memoir, she wrote that he once dropped her on her hip very painfully, and she had the distinct impression that he'd done it on purpose.

What really goes on between two people is very difficult to say.

Gay marriage is legal in Sweden. It has been since May of 2009. So naturally Sven and I had talked about it. Given my professional situation, it wasn't really something that would have been beneficial to us. I'd never been a fan of marriage. My parents split up when I was very young and my mother never indicated any inclination to try it again. I couldn't blame her. When gay marriage became a political issue, of course I was torn: if there *were* legal benefits to be gained, they should be equally accessible to everyone, but I had no understanding of why the state should be interested in whether people were involved in committed sexual or romantic relationships. Aside from the RSB, democratic socialism had been part of the attraction of living in Sweden – this kind of thing really shouldn't even be necessary.

Sven thought I was over-intellectualizing the question because I couldn't deal with my emotions. He's a romantic.

Partner struck me as an ugly euphemism. Euphemism only in the sense that people don't like to talk about sex, so they displace it into some kind of business model. Since I have a distaste for business, I see no appeal to something that sounds like a financial leadership team.

Husband in Swedish is *man*, or *make*. *Partner* in Swedish is *partner*. Or *kompanjon*. I guess that's another euphemism we use in English. It's a little less distasteful to me.

Boyfriend in Swedish is *pojkvan*, which is a combination of *pojk* (boy) and *van* (skilled). I think that's kind of hot.

When I was looking up the sign language for "The Man I Love," I learned that the sign for *man* is a combination of *boy* (skimming the brim of your imaginary cap) and *fine* (indicating the ruffles on your imaginary nice shirt).

In that interview at the Walker Art Center, the one with the young woman who gives you the impression she's wearing braces, John Cage described the relationship between the music and the dance in his collaborations with Merce. He said they didn't want one to take precedence over the other. They wanted it to be about "being together in the same place and the same time." That is, the music and the dance being together in the same place and the same time. But it seems like that was maybe also their domestic ideal. I don't know if anybody can really say whether they managed to do it or not.

I have gotten way off topic.

The rebel moth had posted a partnered dance. There was no man. The moth was dancing with a mannish woman. It took me a minute to figure this out. She was what we sometimes call a "handsome woman" – very striking, with chiseled features and small, bookish glasses. Her arms were bare, and muscular. She was seated in a chair.

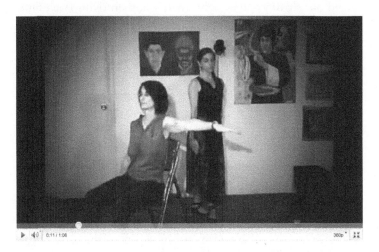

The seated figure didn't really look like a dancer – she looked sort of like she might have been the super of the building, or a neighbor who had stopped by for a chat – but her movement was highly stylized and, while not exactly technical, tasteful and restrained.

The moth had on ballet slippers and some kind of long, dark lacy tutu. Her own movement was vaguely balletic, but her arm gestures recalled something much more functional: semaphore.

You'll recall the original title of my dissertation. I'm interested in this kind of thing.

But semaphore didn't seem to be the only form of communication in the video. That seated figure had a tattoo on her inner bicep – you could see it when she extended her arm. It was a word – I was sure of it – but there was no way to make it out in the dim, low-res video, even when I paused it on full screen.

The two of them were at odd angles, and as in the moth's other dances, their eyes were downcast. The seated dancer made only three moves in the whole piece: when the piano came to a particular small motif, she extended her arm at an angle, and leaned out slightly – first right, then left, then right. Each time, her arm descended unnervingly slowly.

The moth moved much more quickly, her arms alternating in angular movements like the ticking hands of a clock. Her feet shifted in and out in similarly mechanical motion. And each time the seated figure's arms dropped to her side, the moth would lean in wistfully for a moment, and then resume her solitary focus before her.

Their movement only coincided on the very last note of the *Gnossienne*. Skewed away from one another, their breath audible, they slowly raised both arms, simultaneously, to their sides, and slowly let them fall. With conviction and with a rigorous sadness.

They were disjointed, and yet connected, out of sync, and yet together.

I was aware I was projecting.

Of course the rebel moth's two subscribers had let their opinions be known immediately. The carper, as was his wont, was the first to jump in: "Okay, little lady, I see you called in the reinforcements! Nice one, but whats up with the rythm??? Batetment tendu meeds work. Also is taht a boy or a girl???"

Good grief.

I imagine that the moth hesitated before firing back: "Neither Patriarch nor Pussy." She didn't even bother to address the comment about her *battement.*

Touché.

And then, in a subsequent comment, she added, mysteriously: "You'll know Her – by Her Voice."

And then that paragon of sincerity, GoFreeVassals, stepped into the fray, stating the obvious: "I say it is as great to be a woman as to be a man."

Steeped as I was in academic irony, I found his earnestness something of a relief.

quothballetcarper, however, seemed to feel they were both missing the point: "Hellooooo!!! So then WHO LEADS???"

The moth wrote: "He was weak, and I was strong – then – So He let me lead him in – I was weak, and He was strong then – So I let him lead me – Home."

This rang weirdly religious to me. I was getting confused. But not as confused as the clueless carper, who sounded simultaneously exasperated and moralistic. He appeared to have taken the notion of "Home" entirely literally. "Ahem, little lady, who you go home with is none of anybodys beeswax but MAYBE YOUD LIKE TO CLEAN UP UR ACT A LITTLE BIT THIS IS YOUTUBE!!!"

I thought her response gave a little more information than was really necessary (indeed, this was none of my beeswax, and certainly not the carper's): "He strove – and I strove – too – We didn't do it – tho'!"

The sentimental libertarian just sighed: "Ah lover and perfect equal…"

Then somebody called ihatenetnanny popped up, with this comment: "OMFG. I hate NetNanny. x_____x" Like I_ would ever look at Porn! What kind of slut does my Dad think I am?! Slap? That's it? I would FRICKIN MURDER HIM. I feel you're aggrivation. I can barely even bare to go on the computer anymore."

I wondered if that should be tagged as spam.

Then DJFartMeister78 added this little gem: "faggit fagit fagit bitch fagit bitch_ FUCK YOUUU fagit"

I'm not sure if that was directed at the moth, the freer of vassals, or ihatenetnanny. Fortunately when I checked in a couple of hours later, the moth had removed these last two comments. Good call.

I wrote that and then stared for a minute at my computer screen wondering if I should delete them from this novel as well. But as I already told you, I find it hard to lie.

But I began telling you this whole story in order to explain my increasing paranoia regarding the serial deaths of three of the greatest dance innovators of the last century. Merce's *Septet*, you see, was – unsurprisingly – positioned as a related video to falserebelmoth's new addition. I say unsurprisingly because they both featured Satie compositions, and, if anybody at YouTube actually cared about such things, they displayed a certain similarity in spirit, if not precisely in choreographic style. Merce's, admittedly, was more technically refined. Carolyn Brown's *arabesque* is perfect, even by Vaganova's standards. What the moth lacked in technique, I felt she made up for in straightforwardness. The figure in the chair was the picture of understated grace. You can take this with a grain of salt. I had obviously cathected.

The point is, when I toggled over to Merce again, it was with a leaden sense of dread that I registered the most recent comment. quothballetcarper – of course: "Well Merce old man it took awhile but u got urs! You know this DANCE thing is not an easy 'RACQUET' (nudge nudge wink wink)!!! Hope it didnt hurt to much!!!"

As if to add to the sinister tone of the message, I suddenly realized that the carper had added an icon to his moniker: a tiny keyhole figure of a creepy little gloved hand. It had spots on it. wtf?

I have a confession. Bugs Bunny's sister didn't really show me a matchbook with a picture of Siegfried and Roy. I got the idea for that when I was investigating hotels in Las Vegas, because I remembered that cartoon in which Bugs was trying to get to Las Vegas and he made a wrong turn in Albuquerque and ended up in Nazi Germany (oops). I figured maybe his sister would also have wanted to spend some time in Las Vegas, so I started to look up the hotels where she might have stayed. As I went down the rabbit hole, no pun intended, of the Stardust Hotel Google search, I found myself staring at that image from an eBay auction. I got quite absorbed in the story of Siegfried and Roy. I almost ordered a book about their "secret life" from amazon.com, but made do with what was posted on Google books. While on eBay, I was sorely tempted to buy a limited edition Siegfried and Roy commemorative wristwatch originally sold at the Mirage Hotel (only $6.99 buy-it-now, plus shipping). There were also some commemorative white tiger Beanie Babies, but these were very pricey. I spent about three days on this wild goose chase. I told myself it was "research" and might come in handy if I ever wrote the novel I kept threatening to write. This one. While on eBay I did order a set of small plastic deer – the ones that Fang left in my planters. Ask me how much work I got done on my academic manuscript.

Also, while I was Googling, I looked up the semaphoric alphabet, just to see if I could decipher anything from the moth's dance. It didn't make much sense – GFEDEFG, ABCDCBA... There was an H, and a Z.

The only thing that made any sense was that last gesture, the raising and lowering of both arms together. This, evidently, means "error." As in, disregard everything I just said.

GAME CHANGE

I decided to join the NYU gym. It was very close to my sublet and I thought I should probably be getting more of a cardiovascular workout. My slow-motion *barre* exercises were not giving me much of an endorphin charge. Also, I was 46. It seemed like it was time to start thinking about things like my heart, and my arteries.

This was another small perk of my cheap-ass post-doc. Gyms in New York are generally very expensive, especially if they have a pool, but the university affiliation – even my tenuous one – qualified me for a very reasonably priced membership.

I liked that this gym was so functional. I've never been a gym kind of guy. Here, however, most everyone seemed to be, like me, a nerdy academic of a certain age, trying to keep deterioration and depression at bay. We had a forlorn solidarity. It was a slightly different story in the weight room and on the basketball courts, where the undergraduate guys tended to congregate.

The idea of cardiovascular equipment was somewhat offputting to me. There were no windows in this room. It seemed like we were rodents on a treadmill. But after all, even hamsters surely realize they're not getting anywhere, and yet there must be something to it, because they keep going. And indeed, once I started, I became a little obsessive about it. I started with the elliptical machines, and then moved on to the StairMaster.

I liked to take my iPod and listen to music with complicated time signatures. I'd adjust the resistance of the machine so I could maintain my HR (heart rate) at 120 BPM for 20 minutes while stepping in rhythm (5/4, 7/16) to my music. I tried to synchronize my breathing with the beat as well. I would count the rhythm inside my head, but somehow I was able simultaneously to ponder other aspects of my life – embarrassing or possibly insensitive things I'd written or said, the situation with Sven, possible scenarios for a scene in my novel, what I might prepare for dinner.

There was an aging hippie who was there almost every day. His body was wiry and taut. He had a grizzled ponytail, and he would balance a water bottle on top of his head as he extended his arms to the side and pumped backwards on the elliptical trainer with great determination. I wondered what department he was in, and if his colleagues considered him eccentric.

The hippie liked to look into the mirror as he worked out. I tended to keep my eyes shut.

One day I was pumping up and down on the StairMaster, trying to maintain the equilibrium of my tempo, breath, HR, and questions relating to the meaning of my life. I was listening to Philip Glass's *Mad Rush* (7/16). I was pretty sure I was nearing the end of my cardio session. My eyes fluttered open – quite right: the digital clock registered my time at 19:44. As I slowed my pace, my gaze wandered forward toward the row of StairMasters in front of me, and I glimpsed a strangely familiar pair of gleaming white tennis socks, pulled high. I raised my eyes and took in the twill plaid tennis shorts, the carefully tucked-in piqué tennis shirt, and the steely gray hair – holy shit. Just as I made the connection, his head turned, and from behind his browline eyeglass frames, he shot me a withering glance – but followed it with a slight smile. It was Jimmy Stewart – from Zagreb! Here in New York City!

In other words, when I said he was lurking at the scene of

the crime, I didn't just mean on YouTube. He could have been in the city the day it happened. He LITERALLY could have BEANED MERCE. "Hope it didnt hurt to much!!!" The very thought made my blood run cold. And – to make matters worse – that ridiculous miniature tennis racquet was resting against the base of the StairMaster – as if warning me to "mind my own beeswax," as he surely would have put it!

Slack-jawed, I felt myself sinking down toward the ground. I watched as Jimmy took a jaunty hop from his machine, gathered up his axe and walked assuredly out the door. I didn't need the sensors on the machine to tell me my heart. Was. Pounding.

As soon as I got home, I checked in on that Merce video, *Septet*. There were no further comments from the carper, the moth, or the freer of vassals. A couple of people had typed in the obligatory "rip" or "bellissimo," but I saw no clues.

All was quiet on the moth's channel as well. But it felt like the quiet before the storm.

I hadn't merely been looking at Merce on YouTube. I'd also been doing some good old-fashioned book reading. This was not for my own book revisions. Although I'd always found Cunningham interesting, he hadn't figured prominently in my dissertation, which focused on ballet more narrowly construed. Roger Copeland's book-length critical evaluation came out in 2004, and of course I read it then, but hadn't looked at it in some time. I went back over his description of Cunningham's aesthetic. He said that Merce's dancers had "the aura of sangfroid." That was pretty accurate. It rang strangely ominous, though, given the circumstances. Copeland took Moira Roth to task for lambasting Cunningham, Cage, and the visual artists with whom they collaborated as practicing an "aesthetic of indifference." Roth seemed to think the "cool intelligence" of their work made it not only emotionally but also politically detached. Copeland argued that their way of refocusing your attention in fact did have profound political implications.

As for the emotional implications of this aesthetic, I don't think I need to tell you, I have a strong emotional response to understatement. Copeland seemed to have a similar reaction.

It's interesting, it seems Copeland's not gay. He thanks his wife and son in the acknowledgements of the book.

You'd think I'd know that for sure, given how small the field of dance scholarship is. But as I already told you, I generally try to avoid professional gossip.

Copeland also really goes after Susan Foster in that book. He seems to enjoy provocation. When she criticizes the excessive "whiteness" of Cunningham's "chaste" dances, Copeland muses, "Maybe she believes that all African American men have large penises."

Maybe you can see why I keep those see no evil, hear no evil, speak no evil monkeys next to my computer.

But speaking of sangfroid, as in cold-blooded murder, one afternoon that week when I got home from the gym there was a text on my phone from Sven: "got 2 watch woman n d window gr8 tmot." I looked up *Woman in the Window* on the IMDB: Fritz Lang. I'd never seen it, so I popped it to the top of my Netflix queue. Two days later it arrived.

Well, I could see why Sven thought I should watch it: it was about a nerdy, middle-aged New York City college professor named Richard Wanley (Edward G. Robinson). That would be me, I guess. Wanley's family goes away on vacation, and while bumbling around the city alone, he glimpses a portrait of the beautiful Alice Reed (Joan Bennett) in a window next door to his "gentlemen's club." He's staring at her picture when suddenly she shows up beside him on the sidewalk. You see her reflection superimposed on her painting. That's a pretty interesting shot, from a psychoanalytic perspective.

Anyway, improbably, Alice Reed invites the professor up to her place, and her jealous boyfriend shows up and practically strangles Wanley. Joan Bennett passes Edward G. Robinson a pair of scissors and he stabs the guy in self-defense. They spend the rest of the movie trying to cover up the murder, even though Wanley is strangely feeding clues to his close friend, who just happens to be the DA.

Surely the professor's wife and kids could never imagine him getting into this much trouble while they went off on their little family outing. Likewise, I'm sure Sven would have found it highly unlikely that I would end up inadvertently murdering the jealous boyfriend of some *femme fatale*. I also found that a little hard to imagine.

Still, I suppose it could happen. There's a little plot twist at the end of the film. I don't want to spoil it for you. Let's just say, things are not always as they seem, but sometimes things are actually *more* as they seem than they seem.

The "gentlemen's club" in this movie reminded me a little of the Torch Club, which is the faculty dining club at NYU. As a visiting scholar, I was also entitled to dine there if I wanted to. Every once in a while, I'd go there alone, just because it struck me funny. There was an ornate fireplace, and a big violet-colored rug with the NYU motto woven into it: *Perstare et praestare* – persist and excel. Dan Ferguson told me that the graduate students liked to say it meant "pay and pay."

The Torch Club was pretty swank, but it seemed a little incongruous in the context of NYU, a school more renowned for its entrepreneurial savvy and Manhattan real estate holdings than for its ivy-covered clubbishness. So imagine my surprise when just days after our encounter at the gym I spotted Jimmy Stewart in his spotless tennis whites, leaning against the mantle of the

Torch Club fireplace, fondling an unlit cigar as he gamely chatted up the Russian hostess, Galina. She was laughing girlishly at something he'd said. Finally she noticed that I was waiting to be seated and she came over to greet me: "Khello, sir, velcome back to Torsh Cloob." Jimmy looked at me and we both nodded. I was doing my best to conceal my utter panic. Galina led me to a banquette toward the back of the room. I pretended to be reading over the menu, but I looked up furtively to see him make what appeared to be another witticism and leave, Galina smiling and waving him out the door. She blew him a kiss.

I tried to read a little bit of the new issue of *Dance Chronicle* (George Dorris had an article about the early "ballet wars" between the Met and the Manhattan Opera), but of course my mind was racing. First the gym and now my "gentleman's club"... Was he following me? But he'd gotten there first...

I asked for some tea and splurged on a pear *tarte tatin*, despite my increasingly worrisome financial situation. I tried to maintain my cool.

I spent about half an hour nibbling at my tart, sipping my tea, freaking out about Jimmy Stewart and pretending to read *Dance Chronicle*.

On my way out, I asked Galina, as casually as I could, "Excuse me, that gentleman with the cigar and the tennis outfit, he looked very familiar... Is he a faculty member?"

"Ah, sportsmen-professionál?" she asked, smiling broadly. "No, no, he is great atlét, working at NYU gymnasium. And player of – how you say? – гавайская гитара. He is regular here, he is great friend of Duke."

Player of what? At Duke University? I was confused. It seemed that that would amount to something of an institutional disloyalty.

A large party was arriving – it looked like a hiring committee – and Galina had to excuse herself before I could press for any more details.

The next day I found myself staring at the potted plant near my window. It was a rubber tree that was left behind by the regular tenant. It had long woody branches scarred with the nubs where the leaves had fallen off, but then in unexpected places, there were fleshy, deep green clusters of young leaves, and pale-green baby shoots. It looked like a plant that had seen some rough times and come through to tell the tale. This was the plant where Fang had left the two apprehensive little deer standing in the dirt.

I took a picture of one of them with my phone and sent it to Fang. I thought maybe she'd be wondering how they were doing. The deer, like the plant, seemed to be doing okay.

Fang wrote me back a short text, in French: "*ma biche.*"

That got me thinking about the term *biche.* As you may know, it means *doe* in French, but it's also a feminine term of endearment, like *sweetie.* The thing was, the deer that Fang had left in my planters both had antlers. I Googled "can female deer have antlers" and learned the following: reindeer, yes; caribou, yes;

whitetails (deer in question), only rarely, in cases of "excess testosterone." But who exactly determined what was excessive?

Further sleuthing revealed that "*les biches*" is also a term used for lesbians. This may come from the "vaguely lesbian" 1968 film by Claude Chabrol. I'd never seen that. The IMDB suggested a Hitchcock influence, though evidently it's mysterious without really being a mystery, as not much actually happens. I made a mental note to myself to suggest this film to Sven.

"*Les biches*" is also the title of the famous Diaghilev ballet. It was composed (at Diaghilev's request) by Francis Poulenc, and choreographed by Bronislava Nijinska (Nijinsky's sister). It was first performed by the Ballets Russes in 1924. There are certainly implications of lesbianism. The most interesting character is La Garçonne. She was most famously danced – in a royal blue velvet flapper-like tunic with her breasts bound – by Georgina Parkinson in Lord Ashton's 1964 Royal Ballet production. Nijinska was still alive at the time. She explained to Parkinson that La Garçonne should be "an envelope, her exterior neatly folded to contain the information within."

This was Parkinson's most famous role. She said it was difficult for her, because she was, in her own estimation, not much of a technical hot shot. But she had a good feeling for the part.

Despite the obvious distraction of the appearance of Jimmy Stewart, I knew I really needed to focus on the lecture I'd be giving in the fall. I still had a few weeks to prepare, but I wanted it to be good. NYU had what many considered to be the premier faculty in performance studies, including the founder of the field, Richard Schechner. *L'éminence grise.* He was actually pretty friendly. Somebody told me he sat in lotus position at the faculty meetings. I sat behind him at a lecture once and he was sitting normally, but he was making comical sketches of people the whole time in a notebook. I wasn't sure if he'd actually show up for my lecture, but I'd been thinking about him, partly because of Merce.

Merce famously said of his dancers: "They are not pretending to be other than themselves... They are, rather than being someone – doing something." Neil Greenberg, who danced with Merce for years, said he thought maybe Merce rejected theatricality in dance because the roles men were asked to play in romantic ballet felt like a lie to him. As they felt to Neil Greenberg.

But Schechner has a somewhat different way of thinking about the "real" self in performance. He says that there is always a "peculiar but necessary double negativity that characterizes symbolic actions. While performing, a performer experiences his (*sic*) own self not directly but through the medium of experiencing the others. While performing, he (*sic*) no longer has a 'me' but has a 'not not me'... This antistructure could be expressed algebraically: 'not (me... not me).'"

So even if Merce wasn't dancing Prince Siegfried, he was still dancing "not Merce... not not Merce." Or algebraically, "not (Merce... not Merce)."

I mean of course Prince Siegfried of *Swan Lake*, not of Siegfried and Roy.

Georgina Parkinson as La Garçonne was "not (Georgina... not Georgina)."

I came all the way to New York from Evanston to see Neil Greenberg reprise *Not-About-AIDS-Dance* in 2006. The most astonishing moment was when he danced with his face. He was very still. His eyes rolled back and trembled delicately. The text projected above him said:

> This is what my brother Jon looked like in his coma.
> He was in a coma 2 days before he died of AIDS.
> I'm HIV+.

But this part of the dance isn't meant to be about me.

Neil Greenberg probably also thought he was going to die like that when he made this dance in 1994. So he was dancing Jon Greenberg, but also, "not Neil Greenberg... not not Neil Greenberg." Even though he said, "this part of the dance isn't meant to be about me."

On August 8, 2009, a small private plane collided with a helicopter carrying a group of Italian tourists over the Hudson River. All nine passengers in the two vehicles were killed. I didn't actually see the crash, but the view from the balcony of my sublet was such that if I leaned out a little, it was possible to see a small section of the Hudson River between two buildings.

I slept badly that night.

On August 9, 2009, exactly two weeks after the death of Merce Cunningham, the weather was stormy in New York City. The rain and wind made the water of the river choppy, so they had to temporarily suspend the search for bodies.

The search was taken up again on August 10, and the wreckage of the plane, along with the last of the missing bodies, was recovered from the bottom of the Hudson.

That afternoon the sky was still gray, but the rain had stopped. It was a Tuesday. I was having a hard time concentrating on my work.

I was feeling a little worried about Sven.

Like a redeeming angel, Ellen called. Ellen, my massage therapist. Actually, I couldn't really lay claim to being her client anymore. I'd seen her sporadically when I was dancing in New York in that knocking-around period before I lived in Sweden, and we'd remained friends. Every once in a while she'd work a kink out of my neck, but given my limited means on my post-doc, I was no longer in a position to hire her for real bodywork. But she liked me, so she'd periodically call me and try to get me to drive up with her to her friends Randy and Jeremy's place in Woodstock. She kept telling me how relaxing it was, and that we could go skinny dipping, and how Randy knew Joan Acocella because he worked at *The New Yorker*.

I told her I'd drive up with her that Thursday. I thought it might do me some good.

Looking at those plastic deer in the planter, something popped into my head. Antlers. I remembered antlers. They were in that first video of the moth's – the one with the moonwalk. I needed to go back and check her channel.

There was a new video! It had just been posted. It was very different from what had come before. The first thing I noticed was a change in the décor. This video was clearly shot in the same space as her prior dances. But on the wall, hanging next to the portrait of Bruce Lee, there was an electric guitar.

And in fact, this was the instrumentation of the music to which she danced – a heavily distorted, totally psychedelic electric guitar solo, accompanied only by a spare yet resonant bass. It took a little while to register that they were playing Carole King's "Natural Woman."

In keeping with this theme, the moth had let down her hair, both literally and figuratively. It was a little unruly. She'd scrapped the leotard for bell-bottom jeans and a skimpy white top. She looked like she might have had a beer or two.

Her dancing was in no way, shape, or form balletic. She was rocking out. As with her other videos, however, her gaze was mostly directed downward, or her eyes were closed. She'd periodically run her hands over her body in what appeared to be unapologetic autoeroticism. When she ran out of choreographic ideas she started swinging her hair around. It was pretty extreme.

The exhibitionism of her dance seemed entirely in keeping with the musical interpretation, which was, I think, extraordinary.

You will already have surmised from my brief mentions of my musical choices that I'm not really somebody you would describe as a "rocker." Sven's exposed me to a certain amount of pop music, but on my own I tend to listen to classical and jazz. I do have a basic knowledge of the major figures in the history of rock 'n' roll – including Jimi Hendrix, of course. He was the one this music made you think of. What Hendrix did to "The Star-Spangled Banner" was pretty much what this guitarist had done to "Natural Woman." It wasn't an ironic cover. He seemed to want to allow the song to be as rapturous as it could be. Hendrix managed to make a lot of tripping hippies have a moment of understanding the ecstatic possibilities of a national identity they didn't even know they loved. I wasn't there, of course, but I think that's what happened. This was something like that.

Hendrix was right there in the related videos, so soon I was scrolling through Hendrix performances and interviews. Dick Cavett interviewed him about "The Star-Spangled Banner" incident, and Cavett says, as if in his guest's defense, "This man was in the 101st Airborne, for those of you who'll be writing in nasty letters." This confuses Hendrix, who doesn't understand why there would be any nasty letters coming in. Cavett explains that any "unorthodox" interpretation of the national anthem is sure to inspire hate mail.

Hendrix says softly, "It wasn't unorthodox. I thought it was beautiful."

It really was beautiful.

Anyway, scrolling through the various Hendrix offerings, I encountered a song I had, of course, heard before, but I'd never really heard it quite this way.

"When I'm sad, she comes to me, with a thousand smiles she gives to me free. 'It's all right,' she says. 'It's all right. Take anything you want from me, anything.' Fly on, little wing."

My eyes filled with tears.

Little wing. Rebel moth. I took this very personally.

I looked at the ruffles blooming out of the neckline of Hendrix's velvet jacket, and remembered the sign language gesture for *man* – indicating the brim of an imaginary boyish cap, the ruffles of an imaginary elegant shirt. A certain masculine ideal.

Little did I know that the moth's ecstatic duet with the electric guitar was to be a kind of farewell performance. Not that she was going away, precisely, but this dance brought about a profound reaction from her two most vociferous viewers. GoFreeVassals seemed to be unable to contain himself. While his prior messages had indicated, as I said, a palpable erotic tension, this time his response was explicit: "Little you know the subtle electric fire that for your sake is burning within me."

Meanwhile, the new musical selection was clearly viewed by the carper as a provocation – and one that demanded a radical shift in strategy. Apparently, he was miffed to have his position as instrumentalist usurped: "Ohoooo!!! I see ur goin ELETCRIC. Intersting choice. Guess the BATHROOM wasnt quite BIG ENUF????? Fine. This calls 4 a GAME CHANGE. A mans gotta do what a mans gotta do Im outta here, but U R 2!!! Pick ur new HANDLE!!! Freedom Boy, that means U 2!!!!! Signed, ThyMusketEmailJerk" – a fitting moniker for his weirdly threatening and yet anachronistic digital communiqués.

The carper had proposed a game change: if the moth was going electric on him, evidently he wanted to shift the rules, and the names of the players. Of course, that's what's utopian about the Internet, but also creepy – this possibility of jettisoning one persona for another. I would like to believe that it was the liberatory potential of the proposition that led to my friends' acceptance of it. falserebelmoth responded with what struck me as a slightly risqué *joie de vivre*: "Perhaps I asked too large – But smaller bundles – Cram. (AhNethermostFun)" The freedom fighter, likewise, declared his fervor. He was in, come what may: "I have instant conductors all over me… (ACabFreshenerOnTypos)"

There were a couple of other comments from random interlopers. Somebody called heavymedlarruti666 compared the guitarist's solo favorably to Slash. This appeared to infuriate callmelegobob, who wrote: "@heavymedlarruti666 go fuck ur self u bitch slash is much better then most crap u probly listen too fagget now go back_tofuckin ur dad u quier and yes im 10"

This time the moth didn't even bother to delete these comments or mark them as spam: she was evidently ditching the whole channel.

Fly on, little wing.

PART II

Back to the Garden

wo days later Les Paul was dead.

I was in Woodstock the day that Les Paul died. Ellen and I were nearing Randy and Jeremy's house when we heard it on the radio.

So this time I was the one who texted Sven with the big news, but he just answered: "*vem är det?*" I explained that he was the inventor of the electric guitar. Sven acknowledged the magnitude of the loss: "ufb!"

Ellen was also taken aback: "Wow. Les. Paul. It's like the fucking name of the instrument."

But they really had no concept of how hard this news was hitting me, considering the recent emergence of the electric guitar as a singular bone of contention in my alternative YouTube universe. Could the carper – or should I now be calling him the email jerk? – be going to such extremes of retaliation? Had the shift from uke to Les Paul really precipitated the taking up of the musket?

Of course I didn't go into the whole story with Ellen. I just expressed the vague and general disbelief that many people must have been feeling that day. But I had a darker preoccupation. Something felt badly wrong.

I know, I know, Les Paul was 94 and he had pneumonia.

Randy and Jeremy weren't there when we got to their house, but they'd left it open with a note telling Ellen and me to make ourselves at home. To her, that seemed to mean preparing herself a vodka tonic, lighting up a joint, and stretching out on a lawn chair in the backyard. To me, it meant tapping into their wireless connection on my laptop and getting some information.

Les Paul was somebody I knew of but had never paid a lot of attention to. But given the circumstances, I felt compelled to do a little research on him. As you surely know, he's as well known for his talents as an inventor as for his musical gifts. It wasn't just the solid-body electric guitar, either. He pretty much came up with multi-track recording. Some of his ideas came to him when he was very young, horsing around with his mother's radio and telephone parts. I found a recent interview he'd done with *Esquire*, in which he told a story of being sick with the mumps at the age of five: "They threw me in a crib so I wouldn't roll out onto the floor. And there's a big bay window in my house, and that window stayed perfectly still until that train started to chug. At a certain speed, I could reach up and feel the pane, and that glass pane would vibrate. I said, Doggone, there's got to be a reason for this. So I go to the kindergarten teacher, and she takes me to the science teacher, and the science teacher takes me to the library and reads it off to me – 'This is called resonance.' That was the beginning."

Obviously, Les Paul was a genius, but he was always saying things like, "Doggone." Then when I actually started to watch the videos of him on YouTube, I realized that his music was like that, too.

I also read a little bit about his relationship with Mary Ford, who was his wife and musical partner for many years. Her name was Colleen Summers when they met, but he encouraged her to change her name to Mary Ford. Why in the world would you encourage somebody to change her name from Colleen Summers to Mary Ford?

Les Paul was from Waukesha, Wisconsin. So was my mother.

Randy and Jeremy got home around six. They were coming back from the farmers' market. I heard them pulling into the drive. Ellen appeared to have fallen asleep on that lawn chair, so I went out front and introduced myself, and then helped them in with the bags of produce. Randy had clunky black glasses and nearly shoulder-length blond hair which he tucked behind his ears. There was something very youthful and springy about him although I gathered from what Ellen said he was almost my age. He and Ellen had been at Princeton together. Jeremy was a little taller, and marginally less animated, though they both seemed pretty excited.

"Oh. My. God. Can you believe these heirloom tomatoes?!!!" Randy said as he began pulling them from a bag. "Jeremy, take a picture for Facebook!"

Jeremy couldn't find his phone right away so I pulled mine out and snapped this:

"I LOVE THESE!!! YUM!!!" While Randy arranged the vegetables in the fridge, Jeremy began opening a bottle of red wine. Randy asked me how long I'd known Ellen and then told a funny anecdote about a performance art piece she'd done in 1990 at the Princeton Quad inspired by Carolee Schneeman's *Meat Joy*.

"Oh, speaking of performances, you wouldn't believe what you missed at the farmers' market today. Brian Madden and the Neo-Trio – look, we bought the CD!" Jeremy passed it to me: *Bi-Saxual in Woodstock*. Brian Madden plays both tenor and alto. The photo on the back showed three white-haired guys with two saxes, an upright bass, and drums. One of their tunes was called "Mr. Al Fresco, the Outdoors Type." Brian Madden had included some self-effacing comments on the back of the CD indicating that he didn't consider himself to be in a league with the Charlie Parkers and the John Coltranes of the world, but that he hoped he spread a little pleasure by blowing his horns.

Jeremy said that after the Neo-Trio, Phil Void and the Dharma Bums had taken the stage. "Get it? Phil. Void. It's very Zen!"

Randy widened his eyes and looked at me. "Oh. My. God. Ellen would LOVE Phil. We invited him and the Dharma Bums to swing by later."

Jeremy handed me a glass of red wine, and another to Randy. We all tapped glasses and took a sip.

Ellen stumbled in, bleary eyed, and hugged her friends. She filled a large glass with water from the tap and leaned against the counter as Jeremy put me to work shucking corn. As I removed an ear, I noticed a flyer stuffed in the bag, and pulled it out. It was from the Woodstock Farmers' Market Festival: "Super Fire Woman The Roller Dancing Super Hero of The Heart™ will be at the festival on September 2nd to sing an original rap song on her favorite subject, yes you guessed it, love and the power of self love on the main stage at 5:45pm. Tommy Be will be accompanying her on the frame drum."

I was asking myself why I'd dawdled so long in coming to Woodstock.

We had those tomatoes with basil, olive oil, and sea salt. Delicious. Randy grilled some big bloody steaks. We boiled the corn, and Jeremy made a salad. We drank a lot of red wine, and Ellen asked Randy what Joan Acocella was like. She was asking for my benefit, but as I've already mentioned, I'm not a big one for professional gossip. Still, I was enjoying Randy's storytelling.

Then Jeremy began giving us tips about skincare that he'd just learned from Nicholas Perricone and Jessica Wu, the celebrity dermatologists. Jeremy was a journalist, and he did some pretty heavy-duty stories – he'd recently been on the road with Hillary Clinton for a profile in *Vogue* – but on account of his job, he was also privy to some beauty secrets. He'd spoken with several research scientists as well: the truth was, antioxidants and other micronutrients could indeed have a beneficial effect on the skin's elasticity and clarity, but there was no reason to think they could actually be absorbed through the epidermis.

"The moral of the story is," he said, looking at Ellen con-spiratorially, "eat your face cream."

I looked at the remnants of the heirloom tomatoes on my plate and imagined them slathered with face cream.

Later in the evening Phil Void and the Dharma Bums showed up. They played some Grateful Dead tunes and we all drank more red wine. Ellen did an interpretive dance. I got pretty drunk.

Before I went to bed I texted Sven the following incompre-hensible message: "hanging w hippies wish u wr here eat ur face cream xoxo."

He just answered, "?" I was already asleep.

The next day I woke up with a headache and the unnerving sense that I'd been neglecting something.

Ellen was snoring. We were sharing the guest bedroom. She had the bed, and I'd slept on a piece of foam wrapped in a sheet on the floor. That may sound uncomfortable, but I actually like a hard sleeping surface. It was Ellen's basso honking that woke me up. I pulled a t-shirt and a pair of shorts over my underwear and tip-toed out to the living room.

Evidence of the prior night's party was strewn around the house: wine glasses with crusts of wine like dried blood in the bottom, a skanky bong, some pretzels ground into the rug. I looked at the kitchen clock: 7:45. Fuck. I began to clean up, as quietly as possible.

Randy and Jeremy had thoughtfully prepared the coffee maker and left an index card propped against it explaining how to turn it on. I found some ibuprofen in the medicine cabinet of the guest bathroom. After dosing myself with analgesics and caffeine and downing a large glass of water, I settled down with my laptop and got to work.

It will not surprise you to learn that by "work" I do not mean revisions on my academic manuscript. Nor, in fact, do I mean preparations for my upcoming talk at NYU.

I mean Les Paul research.

I found a somewhat informative, short documentary on YouTube. It was narrated by a young woman who seemed to have control of most of the basic biographical facts, but it was a little irksome that she kept mispronouncing Waukesha. She said, "wauKESHa." The correct pronunciation, of course, is "WAUkesha."

Just a day after Paul's demise, the page was already filling up with "RIP" comments, as well as the usual pontificating, gay bashing, and existential philosophizing. Some of this (like my own, above) seemed to have been produced by that Waukesha pronunciation problem.

handdancin	Its not wa-KESH-a,_ its WAH-ke-SHAW.
MaCro1319	R.I.P. i cired when i_ heard he died man i fucking cryd my eyes out lik a little bitch
idahovandal	walk-a-shaw
Necrolokost	Même en France on sait que vous étiez un grand monsieur. Allez en paix_ !

There was a particularly testy exchange between x3min3ntpwnagex and some other musicologists regarding Paul's purported influence on Led Zeppelin which I reproduce here in part:

x3min3ntpwnagex	Maybe its just me, but I don't hear the influence on Pagey. I_ know just about every Zeppelin song there is to know on guitar and I just don't see it or hear it. Page was influenced more by the blues than the jazzy licks from Les.
Grefintiuk	he play very good and original
jdlewis60	On the solo's. Page minces the chords with the leads. Achilles Last Stand is a good example. Though the progression is hard rock, the technique remains the same (no pun intended). Also,_ the speed.
brttfarvroools	faggit u suck dick
beenohopps	she says it funny, where_ hes from. waukesha. its pronounced wah keh shaw. not wa ke sha.

x3min3ntpwnagex	There is still no evidence of Les Paul's sound coming through with Page. He influenced Pagey personally, but didn't have a major effect on the sound of Page's music.
b1llybrown	"Now thats where I heard feedback first from Les Paul. Also vibratos and things. Even before B.B. King, you know, Ive traced a hell of a lot of rock and roll, little riffs and things, back to Les Paul. I mean hes the father of it all: multi-tracking and everything else. If it hadnt been for him,_ there wouldnt have been anything really." Jimmy Page 1977 …stupid boy… i hope you are enlightened, asshole.
wifebeater79	i have the utmost_ respect for this dude cuz if he didn't invent the electric guitar i dont know how i could exist in this shitty world
x3min3ntpwnagex	Well then, enlighten me. What Led Zeppelin songs do you hear_ a Les Paul influence? Also, please let_ me enlighten you. "your" ≠ "you are". Asshole. =)
b1llybrown	your_ an idiot. i hope your kidding.

I wasn't sure if b1llybrown was persisting in misspelling *you're* on purpose.

It was vaguely disconcerting to me that the most heartfelt and least pompous comment on this page was produced by somebody called wifebeater79.

Randy and Jeremy had a place in Manhattan. Usually Randy stayed in the city during the week on account of his job at *The New Yorker*. Jeremy would sometimes go up to Woodstock if he wanted to get some writing done, and Randy would join him on the weekend. This week, though, Randy came up early. The whole town was gearing up for Sunday – they were holding the 40th anniversary of the famous 1969 rock concert. There was going to be a Heroes of Woodstock show that Sunday at the Bethel Woods Center for the Arts, which overlooked Max Yasgur's farm where the original muddy party took place.

Ellen and I had thought we'd just spend one night up there – we hadn't even made the connection about the anniversary – but now Randy and Jeremy were urging us to stay, and after that night of rocking out with Phil and the Dharma Bums, we were sort of getting into the spirit of things. Also, of course, this seemed strangely felicitous to me, given my new preoccupation with distortion guitar. I didn't mention this to my friends.

When Randy and Jeremy got up around 11:00 that morning, I'd pretty much gotten the living room under control. Randy started frying bacon, and Jeremy asked me if I wanted a Mimosa. It was very sweet of him to offer but for obvious reasons I declined. Ellen soon emerged, and of course she accepted.

She asked Randy how far it was to Phoenicia. He laughed and asked her if she had a hankering for a little action with a biker. Phoenicia was just about a ten-minute drive away. It was evidently a slightly more testosterone-soaked corner of Ulster County. But it turned out that Phil had told Ellen about a Buddhist retreat there where they did Reiki. They also had somebody who did craniosacral massage. Ellen wanted to check this place out. She thought maybe she could pick up some body-work clients there, at least on a seasonal basis.

Randy had some gardening he wanted to get done that day, and Jeremy was editing a story on Ruth Bader Ginsburg.

Although I would have been happy to sit in the guest room with my laptop doing more Les Paul research, I thought it might be good to get out of our hosts' hair for a little while, despite their hospitality. I told Ellen I'd go along for the ride to Phoenicia.

Ellen's car was a dark red 1988 Hyundai Excel. The passenger-side door made a slightly worrisome rattling sound when she went over 30 MPH or so. I strapped myself in. She had the radio tuned to Cruisin' 93.5, Good Time Rock 'n' Roll. They were playing Lynyrd Skynyrd's "Sweet Home Alabama." Ellen was driving barefoot and when we got to a light she put one foot up on the dashboard, leaned her head back, closed her eyes and sang, "In Birmingham they love the Gov'nor. Now we all did what we could do. Now Watergate does not bother me. Does your conscience bother you? Tell the truth..." This was weird because Ellen is, like me, a brown person from a northern state. Minnesota, to be exact. I assumed she knew the "Gov'nor" in question was George Wallace.

I said, "You like this song?"

She looked at me sideways and said, "Gray, you take things too literally." I was starting to wonder about the wisdom of driving to a biker enclave in the Catskills with Ellen. I was hoping she was not going to get pulled over by some Phoenicia traffic cop for having her bare feet up on the dashboard. If I knew Ellen she also had some pot in the glove compartment.

When we got to the Buddhist retreat center, the guy at the front desk appeared to be a college intern. He was very young and a little spacey. I wondered if he went to Bard. It seemed likely. The craniosacralist wasn't in that day, although the Reiki practitioner had an appointment that afternoon. Ellen asked him if they ever needed more seasonal staff, but when he explained that the pay was basically room and board and free admission to the spiritual transformation workshops, she just looked at me.

We decided to get lunch in town. One of the main attractions in Phoenicia is a place on Main Street with outdoor seating called the Sportsman's Alamo Cantina. It wasn't entirely clear to me what the relation was between the three parts of that name. Phoenicia is the water tubing capitol of the Catskills, and people also go there to fish, so I thought maybe that's what they meant by Sportsman. But why the Alamo, and why a Cantina? A laminated card on the table said, "At the Alamo you have the choice of ordering from either the Brio's Pizzeria and Restaurant menu from next door or our unique Mexican menu." I found the option of two cuisines confusing. Go Italian, with Brio? Or pretend we were in an authentic Mexican cantina? But there was an enormous wooden sculpture of Davy Crockett right there next to the patio, and though he was smiling broadly, wouldn't his image implicitly be urging patrons to "Remember the Alamo"? We were supposed to do this by eating very mildly spiced Mexican food?

Again, Ellen thought I was over-literalizing. She ordered a Frozen Margarita. She said, "Damn, too bad we're not staying till Tuesday." The menu said that on Tuesday nights they served "$3 Margs."

I just asked for water, and a plain quesadilla. I was a little worried about cash flow. I hadn't anticipated spending the whole long weekend out of town. While Ellen was as broke as me, she was more prone to throw caution to the wind.

I looked up at that enormous sculpture. I said, "Davy Crockett looks like he has an afro."

Ellen said, "Oh my God, you're right. That's so weird."

That's exactly what Sven texted back when I sent him the photo that night: "*som är så konstigt* :O"

Even Crockett's features looked kind of African. Ellen, Davy Crockett, and I appeared to be the only people of African descent in Phoenicia. Actually, I just fact-checked this. According to Wikipedia, at the time of the last census, there were 381 people living in Phoenicia, and .26% of them were African American. I put that through my calculator: that would be one person. I'm pretty sure that wasn't counting Davy Crockett.

After we finished eating, we decided to take a walk down Main Street. There was a boutique for "birders," an "oddity emporium," and a store that sold "nostalgic candies and games." Then we came to another gift shop that also appeared to be catering to day-trippers like ourselves. Ellen and I again paused before the shop window.

If I tell you I suddenly felt queasy, you will surely attribute this to the quesadilla at Sportsman's Alamo Cantina. Or maybe you will agree with Ellen that I just have a tendency to take things too seriously.

In the window of the store were two fake street signs saying, "BIKER BITCH DR" and "BIKES – BABES – BEER." Well, this wasn't really my style, of course, but that's not what was freaking me out. It was the life-size cutout of John Wayne in a ten-gallon hat, modeling an apron emblazoned with the warning: "You can bite a HOG'S ASS if you don't like my cookin'!"

I was looking at John Wayne's face, and despite the cheeky tone of his novelty apron, I felt him gazing deep into my inner being.

He knew something about me. And he was concerned.

Beside him, two other novelty aprons screamed what his pitying gaze implied: "KITCHEN BITCH!" "DON'T MAKE ME POISON YOUR FOOD!" I thought maybe I was going to faint.

I covered by snapping another photo with my phone. Ellen said, "Let's go back to Randy and Jeremy's. It's almost cocktail time."

I didn't even send this photo to Sven.

Friday night we played Bananagrams and Ellen got wasted. Because she kept shouting obscenities and threatening to remove an article of clothing when forced to pick up new tiles, Jeremy suggested we play by the simplified "Banana Smoothie" rules, in which there is no "peeling" or "dumping." This just seemed to further encourage her and before long she and Randy were streaking in the backyard. I thought of Tomislav Gotovac and Vlasta Delimar. Jeremy and I remained inside. He put down "hoc" and said triumphantly, "Bananas!" I challenged him, and indeed, his closing move wasn't recognized as a word in English by the authority on which we had agreed to rely: "hoc, it turns out, isn't in the free Merriam-Webster Online Dictionary, where you just searched." But the page also said, "However, it is available in our premium *Merriam-Webster Unabridged Dictionary*. To see that definition in the Unabridged Dictionary, start your FREE trial now." This was confusing. Was Jeremy a Rotten Banana or not?

We looked at each other. I was tired, and frankly I'm not a particularly competitive person anyway, so I decided to concede. Jeremy was apologetic. It really wasn't such a big deal. We could hear Randy and Ellen squealing in the backyard. Jeremy and I embraced in a sportsmanlike fashion and I went to bed. Just before I turned out the lights, I got a kind of troubling text from Sven: "*Jag är ensam* :-(" I'm lonely. I decided not to answer until the morning. I didn't wake up when Ellen came in. I even slept through her snoring.

Needless to say, Randy and Ellen slept in on Saturday. Jeremy was working in his office. I set myself up on the couch with my laptop and started, ostensibly, figuring out what section of my manuscript I was going to present for my NYU lecture. I wanted to see if I could find a video clip of Forsythe's *New Sleep* on YouTube. It took about a minute to get my answer: no.

I looked at the little "search" box at the top of the YouTube screen.

I typed in: AhNethermostFun.

Bingo.

She'd posted a dance on her new channel. It was another of Satie's *Gnossiennes* – *Lent* – but played on electric guitar in the same psychedelic mode as that "Natural Woman" dance. The sound was extraordinary – Satie's indefinite Orientalism transmuted into a trippy rock 'n' roll dreamscape. The moth's dance was a concentrated meditation, unabashedly, almost embarrassingly sensual. I thought I saw a familiar, faint half-smile on her lips.

The first comment was from ACabFreshenerOnTypos: "the secret shall be told; All these separations and gaps shall be taken up and hook'd and link'd together." Hm. Ironically, his call for disclosure was perhaps his most enigmatic utterance yet.

Nethermost responded, it seemed, with some misgivings about the freshener's proposed candor: "A Secret told – Ceases to be a Secret – then –"

And, though it didn't surprise me, I couldn't suppress a shudder when I saw that the email jerk had immediately crashed this party: "Whooooa there nelly, WHAT IS IT ABOUT _LENT YOU DONT UNDERSTAND??? You know what the duke said: 'SCREW AMBIGUITY. PERVERSION AND CORUPTION MASQUERADE AS AMBIGIUTY.I DONT TRUST AMBIGUTY.' No esriously I cn dig it but I still thnk u need to work on ur turnout. Also I have a dlvery 4 u – Stork Club next weak??B there or b □!!!"

Wow. His typing was really deteriorating. The more distressing thing, of course, was that he seemed to be proposing yet another physical encounter with Nethermost – this time at an extinct but storied nightclub. wtf?

Speaking of deteriorating: so was the level of discussion on that Les Paul documentary video. Somebody had posted something about how Michael Jackson had gotten so much more attention when he died and then everybody and his brother seemed to jump in saying what a "fuckin freak" MJ was and the attention he got compared to Les was a case of "revearse discrimanation" and somebody said, "Let em stick to their jungle boogie music" which was when I started to feel a little dizzy again and I had to get off YouTube.

I texted Sven an anagram of his name: "danger! doves!"
He answered, "thats so weird just watched the birds."
I said, "dodge ravens!"
He said, ":)"
He also said his stomach hurt and I told him to try to eat anyway.

Although I'd mentioned hanging with hippies and I'd sent that shot of the Davy Crockett sculpture, I hadn't actually come out and told him I was spending a few days in Woodstock. I just thought it might make him feel a little left out. He could be like that sometimes. I didn't like to hurt Sven.

The Woodstock reunion concert was only scheduled for one day, although the original festival was August 15, 16, and 17. In point of fact, Hendrix didn't come on until 8:00 a.m. on Monday the 18th, which sounds like early morning, but was actually more like really, really, really late Sunday night. As everyone knows, the 1969 concert was muddy, messy, and somewhat disorganized, though apparently sublime. The 40th anniversary concert was pretty clean but not exactly, at least from my perspective, mind-blowing.

There were some old hippies, of course, and that was kind of heartening. I'd really never seen so much tie-dye.

Jeremy had managed to get us all press passes. This was a good thing because I wouldn't otherwise have had enough cash for a ticket, but it made me feel a little sheepish and as though I really ought to be taking notes. But as I said, I often feel like I'm doing research anyway.

We'd brought a blanket, and we staked out our own little plot.

The legally blind, virtuosic 15-year-old electric guitarist Conrad Oberg opened the event playing a pretty faithful cover of Jimi Hendrix's "The Star-Spangled Banner." His technique was impeccable and everyone was very impressed and also moved, considering his age and handicap. Still, you couldn't help but feel that Oberg's fidelity to the original performance might have deprived the moment of some of its transformative potential. But of course, you couldn't really expect a 15-year-old to attempt to one-up Jimi Hendrix. Also, what the hell am I talking about, "transformative potential"? This sounds like one of those workshops at the Buddhist retreat center in Phoenicia.

I didn't want to be the snarky egghead that day, but really, what did any of us expect? To recapture something some of us had missed and others had surely romanticized in their recollections? In the domain of performance theory, it seems we'd suddenly hit the era of "reperformance" – a proliferation of cultural phenomena actively demonstrating our incapacity to come up with anything as politically or aesthetically appealing as the art we were collectively mourning. Was this interesting, or was it catastrophically boring?

This was my inner monologue, listening to Conrad Oberg shredding derivatively on the stage at the Bethel Woods Center for the Arts. Ellen was standing next to me and I suspect she was thinking more or less the same thing, or at least the part up to "transformative potential," but when the song was over we both just said, "Wow." Randy and Jeremy were both tweeting on their iPhones.

There were several "Heroes" performing that day, i.e., individuals who had actually performed at the original festival. Levon Helm was there, Tom Constanten from the Grateful Dead, and Country Joe McDonald. The band Mountain played, and the guitarist got married right there on the stage. He seemed pretty well preserved, all things considered, and he had on stylish white glasses. His bride looked significantly younger, and she had on a flouncy white wedding gown.

An older lady with frizzy, gray hair in a sundress turned around and said to Ellen and me, "You know, at the original Woodstock two babies were born." There didn't appear to be any births taking place at the anniversary concert, though I did see a couple of very pregnant women.

I already mentioned, I'm not a big fan of marriage, but I admit I sometimes get a little choked up when I find myself witnessing a ceremony. Ellen, however, was having none of this. When the guitarist from Mountain started taking his vows, she just said, "Gross. Let's get some beer."

Randy and Jeremy had disappeared some time ago. I suspected

they might be doing some kind of drug. I thought it was probably just as well that Ellen wasn't in on that action, but a beer
didn't sound that dangerous. She bought a round and later I
reciprocated – tall boys of PBR. I almost never drink beer. It
was kind of refreshing.

When we got back to our spot, Jocko Marcellino from Sha
Na Na was singing a song with Canned Heat. I believe I already
admitted to my relative cluelessness about the history of rock
'n' roll, so some of these names didn't mean a lot to me, but
I certainly knew about Jefferson Starship. Big Brother and
the Holding Company also played. Ellen had to explain to me
that this was Janis Joplin's band, although they didn't actually
play with her at the original Woodstock. Obviously, they were
not joined by her now, but there was a Japanese pop singer
named Shiho Ochi ("of Superfly") that performed two Joplin
songs with them – "Down on Me" and "Piece of My Heart."
Apparently this was being filmed as part of a TV special about
her obsession with Janis Joplin. Shiho Ochi was young and thin
and pretty and she had on a black and white striped outfit with
bellbottoms and fringe. She was also technically proficient and
you could certainly see how much she liked Janis, but somehow
it didn't seem to have quite the right spirit. I'm sure I shouldn't
be grousing about this. After all, what did I really know about
Janis Joplin?

MILK AND COOKIES

*R*eally – what *did* I really know about Janis Joplin? I was still asking myself this question when I got back to New York.

First there were some practical things to attend to. I hadn't asked Fang to check in on the plants because I thought they could take it, but four days in the August heat had done a number on them. I felt pretty guilty, and probably over-watered in an attempt at compensation. When I watered the rubber tree, I had the distinct impression that the little plastic deer were looking at me with something like accusation in their eyes.

This also seemed to be the obvious reading of the text I received from Sven that afternoon: "O_o"

Sven had written me the night before asking where I was and what I was doing. I'd felt too tired to answer.

And then there was my body. Four days with no cardio workout. Four days of too much red wine and PBR. I hadn't even done my *barre* exercises up there.

First things first. After watering the plants, I texted Sven that I was working on my NYU presentation. I didn't really feel this was a misrepresentation. That was after all what I was intending to do when I sat down at my computer. And indeed, I spent a good twenty minutes staring at the introduction of my manuscript, wondering how much of it I could cut and paste into a coherent talk.

Some of the most interesting material was on Jean-Georges Noverre. Noverre's *Lettres sur la danse, et sur les ballets* (1760) remains the authoritative work on the *ballet d'action*, in which narrative dominates. Noverre had no patience with the fetishization of technical virtuosity. This is pretty funny because if it weren't for his insistence on *meaning*, you'd practically say he sounded like a postmodernist – not, that is, a postmodernist when it came to narrative, but choreographically, in his defense of non-virtuosic movement as legitimate dance vocabulary.

In some ways, I suppose my sensibility is a little closer to Noverre than it is, say, to Yvonne Rainer or David Gordon. I consider this a weakness on my part – my attachment to narrative. But I consider it a virtue, my lack of attachment to technique.

Anyway, after a while I got bored and decided to take a quick peek again at that Les Paul documentary.

Oh my fucking God – or as Sven might have said, ":O" The email jerk had been there. And the message he left made my blood run cold: "Hey Les!!! Hows it feel to be UNPLUGGED???"

Obviously, this discovery threw me off my game. I really couldn't concentrate on Noverre while some jaunty loon was running around knocking off the cultural geniuses of our era out of a freakish infatuation with an eccentric, aging would-be ballerina. And who was going to believe my story of a malevolent balletomane? I realized this was going to be a tough sell. I couldn't take it public until I had more evidence.

Fortunately, the email jerk seemed more than willing to supply it.

On August 25, 2009, I was standing in line at Morton Williams. In my basket I had a can of tuna, a bag of baby arugula, a couple of grapefruits, a roll of toilet paper, some English muffins, yogurt, and some fat-free half-and-half. It being nearly the end of the month, this was a necessities-only trip. As I approached the register, I picked up a copy of *The Daily News* and started skimming it. There was a story about MJ. Of course there had been a lot of stories about MJ in recent weeks, but this one popped out at me: the Los Angeles County coroner's office had just ruled MJ's death a homicide, after detecting significant amounts of the sedative propofol in his system. Janet Jackson had made an announcement thanking the authorities for bringing to light the possible criminal involvement of others in the death of her brother. It struck me as sad and poignant that MJ referred to propofol as his "milk." Here they produced a photo of a vial of the stuff, which indeed looked pretty milky. I reflected on the fact that dark secrets and extreme innocence sometimes seem to go hand in hand.

Six days later, I was sitting on a corner banquette in the Torch Club waiting for José Muñoz, the Chair of the Department of Performance Studies. I'd run into him walking his bulldog, Dulce Maria, in the NYU compound. After introducing me to his dog, he graciously said we should have a coffee sometime, maybe before the fall semester began and we all got "overwhelmed."

I said, "How about the Torch Club Monday afternoon?"

I immediately regretted this. He looked like I'd just expelled some enormous glob of snot or goo. I hadn't yet fully absorbed the fact that not all faculty members saw the appeal of my gentlemen's club. But being a gracious person, he said, "Uhh, sure... Gee, the Torch Club... That's an interesting idea... Uhh, what time?"

I suggested teatime: four.

The timing of this encounter – and specifically the date – was strategic. That was the day my monthly fellowship direct deposit was supposed to clear. It was possible that Muñoz would charge the bill to a departmental credit card, but I didn't want to count on that since I'd made the invitation. Especially now that I'd seen his reaction. He was probably also anticipating having to listen to me yammer on about my research. Really, who could blame him? I'm sure "visiting scholars" were a pain in his ass.

Anyway, I'd made the suggestion, so there I was, promptly at four. I told Galina I'd wait to order until Prof. Muñoz arrived. I was reading through the latest issue of *The Chronicle of Higher Education*. I started out just skimming the job listings, but given the bleakness of the market, that didn't take too long. Slim pickin's, as they say. Then I got sort of absorbed in an article about for-profit colleges. Apparently these were the only ones doing fairly well in the current economic collapse. The other trend was that universities, both public and private, were increasingly establishing satellite campuses in parts of the world where there was still a little cash to be squeezed. NYU was really at the forefront of this brave new world: everybody was talking about the new campus in Abu Dhabi.

I was pretty deep into something between a dream and nightmare scenario of myself teaching a dance theory seminar in a gleaming new faux-ivory tower in the desert when I heard Galina's girlish giggle, and I looked up: it was him! Jimmy Stewart! He was carrying a large, rectangular, flat package wrapped in brown paper. He set it down and leaned it against a chair near the fireplace. He made some apparently witty remark, setting Galina off in another round of giggles, and then he took a seat and, to my embarrassed surprise, looked directly at me, smiling slightly and nodding. He then quietly told Galina something, and she glanced at me as well and nodded.

I tried to look back at the article I'd been reading, but naturally my mind was frozen. Seconds later, Galina was standing over me with a plate of little cookies and a glass of milk, "Courtesy," she said, "of gentleman. He says hopes to you will be pleasant." She smiled, and walked away.

Jesus Christ. Milk. He sent me milk.

I looked at him in horror, but he was just sitting there sipping an iced tea through a straw.

José Muñoz came bustling in, apologetic for his tardiness and breathing heavily. I was assuring him that he hadn't inconvenienced me at all, and in the hubbub of our mutual apologies, I didn't even see her arrive. She must only have been there for a few seconds. When Muñoz and I finally settled into our places and I looked up, a diminutive, dark-haired figure was whisking her way out the door of the Torch Club, that rectangular package under her arm. Even from the back, I recognized her immediately: NethermostFun! This was it! The exchange of the "delivery"! "Stork Club" = "Torch Club" – it was a Jimmy Stewart witticism!

The email jerk took a last sip from his straw, stood, tossed a handful of dollar bills onto the table, bowed courteously to Galina, and slipped out the door of my gentlemen's club.

Muñoz was saying, "Gray? Are you okay?" He was chomping on one of the cookies.

I shouted, "I think the cookies are okay but don't drink the milk!"

He said gently, "Don't worry, I'm not going to drink your milk…"

The following week classes began. My anxiety (or perhaps we should just go ahead and call it my delirium) retreated somewhat with the sense of excitement that accompanied the beginning of the academic year. Even at my relatively advanced age, I was still susceptible to that feeling of fresh possibility. And New York is so beautiful in September. One afternoon I was walking home from Morton Williams with my usual small bag of staples and I noticed that Bugs Bunny's sister had parked her walker near the little statue of Fiorello LaGuardia on LaGuardia Place. She was sitting there, sunning herself. She had on a white terry tennis hat and an aqua blue tracksuit.

As I approached her, I waved my arm to get her attention and I shouted, "IT'S BEAUTIFUL OUT!"

She stared at me for a few seconds, then smiled and slyly gestured for me to lean in so I could hear her. She screamed, "WHEN YA SAID IT'S BYOOFUL OUT, YA WEMINDED ME OF A JOKE:

"TWO GAYS AH WALKIN' DOWN FIFF AVENUE. ONE OF 'EM SAYS, 'IT'S NICE OUT.'

"DA UDDA ONE SAYS, 'YEAH, I TINK I'LL TAKE MINE OUT TOO.'"

She smiled again and winked.

I thought that was a pretty good one. I made a mental note to send Sven this joke. I was getting increasingly fond of Bugs Bunny's sister. She also seemed pretty into me.

Fang and I met for a hot dog in Washington Square Park a few days later and she told me that Steve Kurtz was coming in the spring to teach a course on "bio art" and "tactical media." Steve Kurtz was a founding member of the politically trenchant and theoretically incisive Critical Art Ensemble. Kurtz himself had been through a hellish episode of trumped-up charges of bio-terrorism, so I imagine Fang felt a certain sense of solidarity with him, after the "monkey tail girl" indignities she'd suffered. Fang had written him about her filiform wart project. Reasonably, he'd written back wondering if she really wanted to do that to her eyelid. Still, he expressed admiration for her determination and told her he'd work with her on an independent study.

She asked me about what I was going to do for my fall semester lecture. I felt a little embarrassed to say that I'd been getting tired of hearing myself talk about Forsythe so I was thinking of talking about Noverre and narrativity in 18th-century classical dance. Needless to say, my analysis was going to be… Derridean. Fang was pretty polite. She didn't point out the obvious: this was going to be a big snooze for most of the performance studies types, whose taste in dance ran more toward the utterly pornographic Ann Liv Young than Jean-Georges Noverre or even Forsythe, and whose theoretical frame of reference had advanced significantly since 1983, which was about where my own had gotten stuck.

Never mind. That day the sun was shining, the undergrads were draping themselves around the fountain, some kooks were playing guitars and bongos, singing old Beatles songs, and Fang and I were eating hot dogs.

As if on cue, a large group of people appeared with their pet dachshunds. They were adorable. We were so enchanted we didn't even remember to take pictures. Fang squatted down and had what seemed like a very intimate encounter with a long-haired little guy. He was wearing a tiny top hat secured by an elastic band. We weren't worrying in that moment about the dismal academic job market, possible charges of "bio-terrorism," the obsolescence of my theoretical paradigm, the impending disfigurement of Fang's eyelid, the racist, sexist, and homophobic slurs so rampant on the Internet, the burgeoning national backlash against Obama, or the serial deaths of some of the greatest cultural icons of the last century. I wasn't even thinking about Jimmy Stewart in that moment. Or how I was going to make it to the end of the month on my paltry fellowship. Or Sven's reaction to his meds. We were just enjoying the beautiful weather that day in the park, charmed by the little wiener dog in his tiny top hat.

Sven was supposed to come visit in October, but as the date approached he was getting a little nervous because of the stomach troubles he'd been having. His doctor was pretty blasé about it. I didn't want to seem like I wasn't taking his situation seriously, and in fact the thought of nursing him through a rough patch without his regular medical support network nearby was a little intimidating to me as well, but I tried to be encouraging. I said I thought he'd be fine. I told him Forsythe was going to have a piece up at BAM and I could probably get us tickets through André Lepecki who was participating in some sort of talk-back after one of the performances. I told him how nice the weather had been in New York. I also said I missed him, because I knew that would make him feel a little better, and indeed, when I wrote that in a text he answered: ":)" – but in truth, my mind was elsewhere.

I'm not sure exactly where.

I was trying to work on my manuscript, of course, though at this point you don't need me to describe my revision process. It was near the end of September, on one of the first evenings you might describe as "seasonably cool," that I had paused in the middle of a particularly stagnant session of comma migration to get a breath of fresh air on the balcony.

There was a light rain falling, and it was just starting to get a little dark out. I looked across the way at the buildings on the other side of the compound and noticed that there was a guy riding a stationary bicycle on a balcony almost directly across from mine. I'm not sure why, but I felt compelled to take a picture of him on my phone:

I was thinking about the stationary bicycle as a metaphor. Perhaps it will be self-evident that I mean as a metaphor for certain aspects of my existence – most specifically, my writing process. My revisions were obviously not "going anyplace" in particular. I wondered if I could do anything with the figure in that novel I was thinking of writing. Documenting the guy across the courtyard was a way of gathering information for the book I might write. A kind of research. But after I'd taken the picture, I felt a little creepy. I made myself nervous wondering if anybody on the other side had noticed me taking this picture, and if they might have taken a picture of me taking a picture of the guy on the stationary bike.

I also started to feel a little guilty about slacking off myself on the aerobic exercise. I decided to head over to the gym, despite the rain.

When I got to the cardiovascular room, the agile, aging hippie had arranged himself in a reverse position on an elliptical machine with his water bottle balanced precariously on his head. His arms were extended toward the ceiling and he was pedaling backwards with a look of concentration. He had a terry stretch headband wrapped around his forehead and his t-shirt was soaking wet. I found the whole situation somewhat intimidating, although nobody else seemed to be paying attention.

I mounted a StairMaster and plugged into my iPod. I scrolled through my Artists list and paused at Aldo Ciccolini playing Erik Satie. I selected All Songs, and set the iPod on Shuffle mode. I closed my eyes and began to climb, measuring my steps against the anxious notes of *Trois airs à faire fuir: d'une manière particulière*. The tempo of the piece was varied, and I found myself alternately scampering and skulking.

For the next twenty minutes, my heart was pounding at the recommended rate of 120 BPM as my mind raced through a course by now all too familiar to me and, I'm sure, to you: the shadowy corner of Nethermost's YouTube interior, her fluorescently lit bathroom filled with the homey plucking and crooning of the nefarious ballet carper, the mahogany-paneled splendor of the NYU Torch Club reverberating with Galina's infatuated giggle, and the various stark and steely pathology labs where I imagined emotionless professionals in medical garb solemnly prodding and puzzling over the ice-cold limbs of Michael, Pina, Merce, and Les.

Even after I dismounted the StairMaster and unplugged myself from the iPod, my heart continued pounding. I stretched a little in the dance studio and then hurried home to check in on my moth.

Living creature, vital dancer! She'd posted another dance – again partnered, but this time by an adolescent boy. Actually, he appeared first, though it was unmistakably her living room. The post was titled *celebrate the body electric*, and it began with a single, reverberating electric guitar as the skinny, shirtless, mop-haired kid wandered, apparently stoned, into the frame. As the guitar ramped up, Nethermost slowly edged her way in from the other side. Her long hair was unbound, and she was dressed, somewhat age-inappropriately, in a little denim skirt and high-tops. They both stumbled toward each other, eyes downcast, as the music collected speed and direction. Suddenly a drum began pounding, a high-pitched, girlish voice began squeaking, the two dancers began hopping, and then all hell broke loose!

The song was nonsensical, epic, symphonic, and weird. For a moment there seemed to be a kind of a chant, which I think I deciphered as "Away we go now!" But it could have been "A baby girl now!" or even "Oh lady, hoedown!" As the bass drum thumped, Nethermost and her lanky friend jumped and flailed. There was a spastic, shrieking explosion, provoking a total choreographic paroxysm, and just as suddenly the pounding drums evaporated – poof – and there was just a shimmering of guitar strings as that uncanny, child-like voice swooped down and up in noteless glissandos punctuated by something like hiccups. The dancers floated on that eerie plane, responding to each gurgle and yelp with a corresponding shudder, a toss of hair, or a flick of the wrist. Then slowly the drum began its persistent thump again, and soon they were hopping and pouncing with abandon, jerking to and fro with each dramatic, electrified howl. The music crescendoed into a chorus of voices both human and instrumental: "Ah-ah-ah-ah-ah-ah-ah-ahhhh!" The dancers joined in the anthemic, ecstatic cry, repeated nine times, at the end of which the moth and her young friend smilingly embraced.

As they walked apart he reached his long, skinny arm to the camera and switched it off.

It seems she'd posted this just two days before, and the only comments thus far were from the usual suspects. The email jerk had perked right up, as usual: "THE HIGH AND THE MIGHTY!" Indeed, they both looked pretty high. I guess by mighty he was referring to the kid, who was skinny, but certainly had that raw energy of youth. Actually, she was pretty energetic, too.

ACabFreshenerOnTypos answered: "Other lands have their vitality in a few, a class, but we have it in the bulk of our people." I couldn't really tell if that was a rebuff to the jerk, or a nod of agreement. *Bulk* was a funny word to use, given the individuals in question (scrawny). It was also odd that despite his new moniker, the freshener typed with exemplary precision, at least relative to your typical YouTube commentator – and certainly in contrast to the jerk.

Then Nethermost inserted the most alarming comment in the thread: "A Death blow is a Life blow to Some."

I shivered. There seemed to me only one reasonable interpretation: she knew about Jimmy and that "racquet" of his – and she was determined to stand up for the side of the Living. If he was out there playing whack-a-mole with the creative genii of our time, she would defiantly headbang in the celebration of youthful vitality.

I could almost feel the irony dripping off his next comment:

"Hm, its like the duke said, tomorow is the most impotrant thing in life. Comes into us at midnight very clean. Its perfect when it arrives and it puts itslef in our hands. It hopes weve learned something from yestrday." Was that a threat? A rebuke? His words had the creepy moralism of a judge at the moment of sentencing.

Then he added, in a separate comment, as if an afterthought and a warning: "SPEAKING OF WIHCH WERES THE DUKE?!REmember talk low talk slow and dont say to much."

This exchange plunged me back into a state of low-grade psychosis which persisted over the next several days. I found myself lurking around outside the Torch Club, pretending to be waiting for someone or composing a text on my cell phone. I was really waiting to see if Jimmy would come by. Not that I knew what I'd do if he did. I also found myself opening my eyes and looking around every few minutes while climbing the StairMaster at the gym. When doing my *barre* exercises at home I'd look across the way at that balcony with the stationary bicycle, though I never again saw the rider.

Sven had gone ahead and bought his plane ticket. He was arriving October 8, which was soon. Lepecki generously got us passes to see Forsythe's *Decreation* at BAM on the ninth. I ordered a couple of movies for us to watch from Netflix. I bought some knäckebröd at Dean & Deluca.

That was the only thing I bought at Dean & Deluca. My financial situation was bleak.

My short-term cash flow was the least of my worries. I really needed to figure out what I was going to do when my post-doc ran out. I'd only dug up a couple of tenure-track jobs to apply for, both long shots, but I knew of some other fellowships I could go for that might stretch me out for another year or two. The MLA job list was already out. A couple of additional opportunities might materialize in the next few weeks, at least if past years were any indication. But then again, this year wasn't really like past years.

Dan Ferguson told me there was an Academic Jobs Wiki that I could sign up for. He told me, though, that it wasn't for the faint of heart. People applying for the same job would post news to the Wiki if they'd been asked for follow-up materials or invited for an interview. That way, if you were up for the same job and hadn't heard anything yet, you could be pretty sure your ship was sunk.

I hadn't yet registered myself on the Wiki, but when I took a look at it, I noticed there were a couple of other links. *The Chronicle of Higher Education* had a discussion forum called *Leaving Academe*. I took a look at it. Somebody named "grey-eyes" said s/he was wondering if s/he might be able to get any "management and consultation" work from his/her humanities PhD. Some MBA types scoffed at this suggestion, and some-body named "untenured" said, gently, that while greyeyes surely had a lot to offer, corporations might not leap at the chance to give him or her work as a consultant if s/he actually had no business experience.

untenured ended his/her post, "Sorry to be a mega downer."

Somebody else gave a helpful citation from a book called *So What Are You Going to Do with That?: A Guide to Career-Changing for M.A.'s and Ph.D.'s:* "One of the most common mistakes made by career-changing academics is confusing their dissertation with their vocation."

I killed an hour or two combing through these disheartening bits of advice.

Then I got back to work trying to excise a few more of those extended endnotes from my manuscript. I was trying to remind myself during the exercise that what I was grimly hacking away at was not my "vocation."

I took a break at one point, stepping out on my balcony. I looked west toward the Hudson River, which was barely visible. Every once in a while I could catch a glimpse of a big ship passing by very slowly.

When I was doing that Merce Cunningham research on YouTube, I'd come across one interview in which Merce mentioned that you could very clearly see the Hudson from his studios on West Street, and that sometimes he'd look out the window while he was teaching class and see a big tanker moving by extremely slowly. He said sometimes when this happened, he'd try to time the particular exercise he was teaching to the time of the ship passing by. He said he never told his students that that was what he was doing. They just went along with his direction and danced very, very slowly.

I looked across the way again at the stationary bicycle. I wondered if I couldn't incorporate something about this anecdote of Merce and the tanker into that novel I was thinking of writing.

Later that night I checked back in on that video that the moth had posted. The cab freshener had popped in again to leave what looked like an expression of frustration or anxiety: "Enough O deed impromptu and secret."

To which Nethermost had responded: "Big my Secret but it's BANDAGED—"

Which prompted this tender conciliatory message from the freshener: "I resign'd myself To sit by the wounded and soothe them…"

Then somebody named Justinsmokes6 piped up with: "wanna make out?"

It wasn't very clear whom he was addressing. Maybe everybody.

Anyway, his interjection seemed to provoke that braggart the email jerk: "OH TRUTH OR DARE IS IT?!! OK I GOT A SECRET. WHEN IT CAME TO KISSING, HARLOW WAS BEST."

wtf?

Sven seemed okay when he arrived. He was tired, but he'd had a long and grueling trip. He has trouble sleeping on the plane. His hair was even longer, and it made him look very young.

I met him at the airport in Newark and we got the NJ Transit train to the city. He just had a carry-on bag. I knew what was in it: seven pairs of carefully folded boxer-briefs, socks, three tank tops, three dress shirts, a sweater, dress pants, a Stieg Larsson book, some sock-weight yarn and double-pointed bamboo knitting needles, meds, condoms, and a few travel-size cosmetics in a Ziploc bag.

I kept a big bottle of contact lens solution for him in my bathroom so he never had to bring any. I think he also liked knowing that the contact lens solution was there even when he wasn't. I don't wear contacts. I did start wearing reading glasses a few years ago.

That first night we stayed in and I cooked. I made Indian food from a Madhur Jaffrey cookbook. I put candles on the table. After dinner we had a long cuddle and listened to Blossom Dearie.

That night he fell asleep pretty early, but around 2:00 a.m. I heard him moaning in his sleep. I think it was his dreams.

The next evening we went to BAM to see the Forsythe piece. It was based on an essay by the poet Anne Carson. Sven and I had nosebleed seats. The dancing, of course, was pretty amazing. Forsythe's movement had morphed progressively away from a recognizable ballet vocabulary, and at this point the convulsive qualities were the dominant ones. Balletic references were like little tics of seeming civility that would pop up out of habit in the middle of all that flailing. The language was somewhat like that as well. It was a little difficult to decipher what, exactly, the piece was "saying." There was a woman (Dana Caspersen) apparently freaking out about love and betrayal. "Is this it?" she wailed at one point. "The fighting, the lying, the affairs?" The voices of the speakers were sometimes distorted electronically, as if to represent sonically the distortion and monstrosity of the things people say to each other in these situations.

Peter Boenisch had published an essay on "ex-scription" in Forsythe's work. I'd cited it in my manuscript. He took this idea from the philosopher Jean-Luc Nancy. He said that Forsythe had his dancers "unwrite" their bodies. This seemed to be related to Anne Carson's ideas about "decreation." The article also cited Agamben on the function of "gesture," which he differentiates from both acting and producing: "What characterizes gesture is that in it nothing is being produced or acted, but rather something is being endured and supported."

That also seemed to be a fairly apt description of what constituted "love" in this piece. It was, as "untenured" might have put it, a mega downer.

This piece was not an ideal "date night" performance. Fortunately, most of the content appeared to go over Sven's head. Or he may have been pretending not to make any connections to our own relationship, as I was.

Of course, the shrieking accusations and floundering gestures flying between Forsythe's dancers bore no audible or visible resemblance to what went on between me and Sven, ever. We are very understated. And neither of us is jealous. We agreed from the beginning that things would remain open. This got a little more complicated when he got that unexpected test result.

I wasn't angry.

Forsythe's dancers were virtuosic but they were not going for what you'd call "beauty." There was nonetheless a poignant *pas de trois*. It was the quietest moment in the evening.

When we were leaving BAM, Sven said, "I liked the trio."

I agreed.

I was kind of hoping we'd run into Bugs Bunny's sister that week so I could introduce her to Sven, but we didn't. We did some walking around the Village. We went to some galleries in Chelsea.

Most of the time he felt all right. The main problem was his dreams.

We got a copy of *Time Out New York* to see if there were any interesting museum shows up. Of course, I felt a certain frisson when I saw there was a photography exhibit up at the Brooklyn Museum called "Who Shot Rock & Roll," but I wasn't really going to suggest that we go to see it. Sven wanted to go to the Luo Ping show at the Met.

Luo Ping was an 18th-century Chinese artist who is best known for an enormous scroll called *Ghost Amusement.* Luo said he could see ghosts, and he painted them. He developed a special technique that involved pouring water all over his paper and then painting on the wet surface with ink, which makes the figures appear to be dissolving before your eyes.

I was especially drawn to one section of the scroll depicting two of these ghosts. They resembled a couple of losers walking on the beach. One was fat with a slightly misshapen noggin and sparse, scraggly hair. The other was skinny but had a flabby belly that he seemed to be clutching. He was wearing a fishing hat. They both had on shorts. They really didn't look like they were painted in the 18th century.

Some of the other ghosts weren't quite so comical. Sven was staring for a while at two skeletons. Later we read that Luo probably based his skeletal images on Andreas Vesalius's *De Humani Corporis Fabrica*, an anatomy book published (in Europe of course) in 1543. I just had to look it up again to verify the title and the date. The strange conjunction of centuries and continents, anatomy and mysticism, fat ghosts and skinny ones, was both bewildering and reassuring.

When we walked out of the Met onto the steps, I felt like we were also dissolving into the scenery.

During Sven's entire stay, I avoided mentioning my furtive YouTube investigations, the moth, Jimmy Stewart, the weird lyrical outbursts of the cab freshener, or my evolving theories regarding the timely or untimely ends of several artistic icons. I also failed to mention my weekend in Woodstock. He never asked any questions about the photograph of Davy Crockett's afro, or that weird comment about eating face cream.

For his part, he mildly declined discussing his thoughts on that FOTO treatment option.

On Sven's last evening in New York we decided to stay home and watch one of those Netflix movies. We chose *I Want to Live!* with Susan Hayward. It was loosely based on the story of Barbara Graham, "Bloody Babs," a hard-boiled floozy who was executed for murder in the 1950s. In the film, she's the kind of big-hearted gal who'll take the rap for a john. After a life of prostitution and petty crime, she falls for a guy, gets married, has a baby, realizes her husband's a dope fiend and then leans on two male "friends" who end up fingering her on a murder she didn't commit. She meets another hottie named "Rita" in prison who seems to want to help her out with an alibi (lesbian overtones), but she's as untrustworthy as the rest. There's a sympathetic journalist who wants to help, but there's not much he can do. Barbara Graham ends up getting gassed.

Most people agree that the film's portrait of Graham is highly sympathetic, and probably inaccurate. The real Graham seems to have cracked an old lady's skull open with a pistol.

The timeline of the film is the weird and brilliant thing. Years of Babs's wayward youth whiz by. So does her marriage and motherhood (in real life, Graham had a few marriages, and a few babies). The botched robbery in which the old lady gets clipped (by somebody else) is a mere blip on the screen. But the last half of the movie practically takes place in real time.

Barbara Graham has been sentenced to the gas chamber and she's waiting to die. There's some question of the possibility of her sentence being commuted. She's hanging around in a cell smoking cigarettes and waiting for the phone to ring. She gets a reprieve of a few hours. That just stretches things out and makes them more unbearable. There's a priest who says some generally unhelpful things. People keep looking at the phone. There's a homely female nurse who grouses about how disappointing men are while smoking cigarettes with Bloody Babs. When it's time to go, Babs asks for one of those satin eye-masks so she won't have to see all the people watching her die.

Then they take Barbara Graham into the gas chamber and strap her into the chair. They strap her around the chest, around the waist, around her arms, and around her legs. You see one of the executioners hooking up the tubes that will lead to an external stethoscope so they can tell when she's dead. The guy discreetly whispers to her to count to ten when she hears the pellets drop into the liquid, and then to breathe in deeply, because that will make it "easier."

She says, "How do *you* know?" Her voice is dripping with sarcasm. He pats her on the shoulder.

Then a lot of people gather around and look in the windows

of the gas chamber. There's a shot of the telephone, as if to say there's still a chance somebody will make the call and commute her sentence, but nobody does. There's a shot of the priest reading the Bible. There's a big ticking clock on the wall. Somebody looks at it, and then gives the nod. You watch another guy open the tanks. You see and hear the pellets drop into the liquid and start to fizz. You count. You watch her breathe. Her head bobs. Then her head swings back. Then it bobs forward again. You watch her hand grip the armrest. You watch it relax.

Sven and I didn't really talk about this movie. We went to bed early that night so Sven would get enough sleep before his long flight.

SINGULAR PLURAL

The rest of October was pretty quiet.

A couple of days after Sven left, David Rousseve presented a dance-for-film project in the department. It was melancholy and a little disturbing. A few days later I saw Felicia McKenzie again in the laundry room. She didn't seem to recognize me. Dan Ferguson had a Halloween party at his place in Astoria. I went as Charlie Chaplin. Fang was a finger. Dan was a rabbit in a hat. Somebody went as a "Body without Organs" (BwO). There was also a very convincing smurf.

I didn't make a lot of progress on my academic manuscript.

On November 1st, I got an e-mail from the woman I was subletting from. She was an anthropologist on sabbatical in Quito. She politely asked me to make sure my December rent check was going to clear before I deposited it for her. There had been a minor glitch in October.

I also got an e-mail that day from the administrative director at the Department of Performance Studies, Ramon Gonzalez, telling me that he was sending out an announcement to the listserve about my talk on December 16 and I should let him know if I needed any kind of technical assistance. Mine was the last talk of the fall semester, and the departmental holiday party would immediately follow it.

Fuck. Excuse my language, but I really had to bite the bullet and figure out what I was going to say.

That evening was the opening ceremony of Performa 2009, the biennial performance art festival run by RoseLee Goldberg. The festivities were supposed to start at 8 p.m. in Times Square. Arto Lindsay, the sound artist, had collaborated with the choreographer Lily Baldwin on a kind of parade. Fang and Dan wanted to go. Times Square had always made me feel vaguely allergic (literally – sometimes I'd break out in hives), and I really felt I ought to be working on my talk, but I agreed to meet them anyway at John's Hot Dog Cart on the corner of 46th and Broadway at 7:45.

Fang is petite but she can really put away the hot dogs. While she was wolfing down her third, Dan explained to me that the piece we were going to see was called *Somewhere I Read…* The event incorporated about 50 dancers moving through the public walkways of Times Square. As you surely know, this is one of the most densely commercial zones of the city. My allergy probably had something to do with this. It's not just that I didn't have the cash to participate in all that consumption. I found it aesthetically overwhelming.

Dan told me that Lindsay had composed the score for the performance to be played on the dancers' cell phones. When we wandered into Father Duffy Square, where they have that TKTS booth, it took us a minute to figure out that things had already started. The performers were scattered around the illuminated steps. They were all dressed in tidy, belted, beige trench coats and they were waggling around their cell phones. Slowly, they began to assume a more uniform pattern of movement. Baldwin's movement vocabulary was markedly pedestrian, even though all the performers had been culled from dance studios. The score, when we finally heard it emanating from the phones, was really very quiet. Sometimes you could hear almost nothing coming out of the phones, but the range of sounds, when audible, was varied – from the percussive to the slightly melodic to the squeaky and mechanical. The movement was correspondingly eclectic. Despite the fact that it was taking place in the national epicenter of theatrical overkill, one could certainly say that the general aesthetic of the piece was one of understatement. I snapped a photo on my own phone.

I heard a couple standing behind me talking about what was going on. The woman said, "I think it's one of those flash mobs. It's probably an ad for those cell phones."

That seemed like as plausible an interpretation as any other.

We stayed until the end, following a cluster of dancers that moved south for a block or so, attracting a mix of disgruntled, enchanted, bored, and mesmerized responses. Finally the dancers lined up to dump their phones, one by one, into a heap, and they dispersed into the crowd.

Fang and Dan and I kind of shrugged. We liked it, sort of, but we weren't sure why. Fang had a stomachache (no surprise) so she left in a bit of a rush. Dan had a friend who was a chorus member in *Wicked* and he was going to hang around the Gershwin Theater until his friend got out. I decided to walk home, down Broadway. In the thick of things, under those enormous, illuminated billboards, I felt dwarfed, but as they receded behind me, I began to feel my normal size again. I was very glad to get down near 14th Street.

I texted Sven that picture of the dancers with the cell phones. He said, " : / "

Five days later I was doing my *barre* exercises to Miles Davis's *Kind of Blue*. I was avoiding revising my manuscript and pulling together my lecture. I was also thinking about modality in music, and ballet positions.

Sometimes, of course, I feel pretty embarrassed of my formalism. I don't mean my good manners, although I am pretty genteel. I mean my preoccupation with form, aesthetically. It's not exactly fashionable. But just as I was thinking about this, Fang called to say that Marjorie Levinson was giving a talk over at CUNY that evening and she asked me if I wanted to go. I asked her who Marjorie Levinson was and she said she'd written a very influential article in the *PMLA* on the "New Formalism." I asked Fang what that meant and she said that renewed preoccupation with form manifested itself in ways both radical and conservative. I asked Fang if she considered herself a New Formalist and she said, "Oh, of course," as though this were self-evident. No need to ask if she were in the radical or conservative wing of this movement.

I hadn't really thought of the filiform wart project as formal in its concerns.

I wondered if you could be a filiformalist.

I said sure, I'd go to the lecture with her.

Marjorie Levinson's lecture was one of the plenaries for a conference on Romanticism and the city. The title of Levinson's talk was listed in the conference program as "Clouds and Crowds, Solitude and Society: Revisiting Romantic Lyric," but it turned out she'd settled on a different one: "Of Being Numerous." I found it a relief that even somebody like her could apparently leave some aspects of her talk to the last possible moment. But she was very impressive. She talked about form as it's thought about in various other disciplines, like cognitive science and systems theory. She gave the impression of knowing what she was talking about.

There was a young woman seated next to me who kept typing away on her laptop as Levinson spoke. I think she was an academic groupie blogger. I was staring at her screen – it didn't seem to bother her. She typed:

> Representation's most "significant" (haha) function, Levinson pointed out, is not to assign a signifier to some readily cognizable signified, but to have that signifier stand for something which can *only* be cognized as a representation. Kant's mathematical sublime served as one illustration, the sublime (or, in mathematics, the infinite) figuring as the representation of a failure in representation. The end-product of this representation, though, is a way of being-singular. The regime of resemblance, on the other hand, captures an ontics of being-numerous. Nothing exists in itself, but only in resemblance to other things (an arbitrarily large set of other things)—through proximity, emulation, analogy, and something I'm not remembering. Somewhere Spinoza and Deleuze/ Guattari make their way in there.

I also got lost during the segue from Spinoza to Deleuze and Guattari. I was just spacing out for a minute. Levinson had quoted that line from Wordsworth, "I wandered lonely as a cloud..." I was remembering that strange sensation I'd had walking down Broadway after the Performa event.

At the end of the talk, Fang asked a very intelligent question about Jean-Luc Nancy's notion of the "singular plural" and what it had to do with an unending situation of war. Actually, it was more of a comment than a question. She phrased it very politely and deferentially, but it was smart, slightly off-topic, and a little intimidating. I remembered Fang telling me that before she realized she wanted to be a conceptual artist, she thought she wanted to be a lawyer. She'd probably make a very good lawyer, though I suspect she'd have to tone down the scrumbling look.

The next day I was having my coffee and reading the paper when I got a text from Randy. He was at Lennox Hill Hospital.

Ellen had tried to kill herself.

Randy and Jeremy had been driving to Woodstock on the evening of Marjorie Levinson's talk when Randy heard a disconcerting voicemail Ellen had left him asking him to look after her cat if anything happened to her. They tried to call, to no avail, and shortly before they got to their house they decided to turn around and check in on her at her apartment on the Lower East Side. After banging on the door for a while, the super let them in, and they found her slumped over the table. She'd taken a bottle of Percocet she'd bought off the Internet. Fortunately she'd vomited most of it up. They called an ambulance and Randy went to the hospital with her. Jeremy and the super stayed and cleaned up.

When Randy and Jeremy busted into the apartment, the cat was just walking around as though nothing had happened.

Randy told me visiting hours started at 11 if I wanted to come by. I got there a little early, and the two of us sat for a while in the lobby waiting. Somebody wheeled an ancient crone out in a wheelchair. He parked her right next to me as he went out to hail a taxi. She leaned over toward me and hissed, "Old age is not for sissies!"

I said, "So I've heard."

She said, "I hate it!" She looked genuinely pissed off.

I thought of Bugs Bunny's sister. I hadn't seen her in a while.

When we went up to see Ellen, the nurse was very chipper. She admired the daisies I'd brought. Ellen looked about like she usually did after a night of excess, except she was in one of those standard-issue hospital gowns and she had an IV for fluids. The three of us made some slightly acerbic jokes, but occasionally Ellen would tear up and wipe her eyes with the back of her hand. Then three other friends of hers from yoga showed up in the doorway, and Randy and I kissed her on the top of the head and told her to call us if she needed anything. He'd gotten a key and promised to feed her cat.

Obviously, this experience derailed me from my work.

I was extremely sad that week.

I also kept thinking about that performance piece in Times Square. I decided to look on YouTube and see if anybody had put up a video of it. The official Performa site had posted one of the event itself, and another of an interview between RoseLee Goldberg and Arto Lindsay talking about it. She was asking him about the origins of the piece and he mentioned that years ago he had spotted Greta Garbo walking around Midtown in a trench coat and dark glasses. He seemed to be relating this to isolation and the cell phone, the way we move through the city in such a self-contained way.

"I vant to be alone."

Both Goldberg and Lindsay noted the possibility of spectators perceiving the piece as an advertisement – Lindsay suggested "a poor man's Banana Republic commercial" – though as I said, the woman I overheard thought it was an ad for the cell phones. That's when Lindsay invoked Garbo, and "wanting to be alone," which was interesting, given the number of performers involved. He also expressed enthusiasm over the fact that the initial call for dancers elicited "groups of friends – which was nice." But I thought the question of what kind of affective relations the dance was meant to create with spectators was entirely suspended. Lindsay and his collaborators seemed content to teeter-totter on the brink of oppressive commercialism, allowing costume, sound, and choreography to simultaneously evoke and lampoon the flash mob – a genre of indeterminate political significance at best.

In the heart of a consumerist paradise/inferno, the intentional understatement and discretion of the performance were what made it seem both critical of and complicit with that consumerism.

You will find this, perhaps, an over-intellectualization of the event. Indeed, but this was what I was trained to do. This, and *pliés*.

I already told you about how sad I was, about the hives I sometimes get when I go to Times Square, and about my walk home after that performance, when I wandered lonely as a cloud.

It will not surprise you to learn that after watching the Performa videos on YouTube I couldn't resist checking in again on AhNethermostFun. I'd been avoiding her channel, knowing it tended to provoke my paranoid delusions. I felt it also contributed to my academic procrastination. But this experience with Ellen had left me feeling tender, and I found myself concerned for the moth as well. I breathed a sigh of relief when I opened her page: she'd recently posted another dance! It was Satie again, another of the *Gnossiennes*, but this time played on distortion guitar and electric bass, sounding much like that earlier "Natural Woman" rendition. The moth was partnered again, but this time with an older gentleman. He was concentrated, delicate, and elegant, and both he and the moth danced with their eyes closed, as if trying very hard to savor every note of the haunting melody. He was wearing some kind of leather pouch around his neck. She had on a Che Guevara t-shirt.

In her description of the dance, the moth had written a peculiarly threatening little note: "To foe of His I'm deadly foe – None stir the second time On whom I lay a Yellow Eye – Or an emphatic Thumb."

The cab freshener had answered, beautifully but obscenely: "phallic thumb of love."

I was mildly scandalized.

And the email jerk? Surprise. He was confusing, touching, and terrifying, all at once: "OH OKAY I GET IT ITS LIKE THE DUKE SAID (HEY WEHRE THE HECK IS HE ALREADY???): IM A GREDY OLD MAN_LIFES BEN GOOD TO ME AND I WANT SOMEMORE OF IT. OKAY HES GOOD 2 GO BUT KEP AN EYE ON THAT GURLY BOY!!"

I wondered if he was making reference to that last *Gnossienne* – the one with the handsome woman. But perhaps you'll understand why I also took this warning personally. And as if to drive home my concern, that vicious Favre fan brrtfarvroools piped in: "fegget faggte fagget bitch byatch fagget suck my weenie!!!"

They let Ellen go home on November 8. I went to pick her up at the hospital. She was acting like everything was just fine, going off about how great her new meds were and how she couldn't wait to get some decent sushi. When we opened the door her cat came over, looked at us, and walked away. Ellen smiled wryly. "Somebody missed me…"

But her place was warm and cozy. She put Erykah Badu on the stereo. I made her some chamomile tea. Randy was also going to stop by after work. I didn't want to make her self-conscious by asking too much, but eventually she just said, "Gray, I'm good. You can go now. I kind of want to take a bath. Dude. I love you." She said it as though I were the one who needed taking care of. We had a hug and I headed out.

I stopped by Economy Candy on Rivington Street, which I'd often do when I was in that neighborhood because Sven liked Beeman's gum and it's about the only place you can get it. I don't even remember when he first had it, but he liked it when I'd bring him some. Economy Candy is a little overwhelming.

Just in the gum section of the "old time favorites," they have Chiclets (bulk and in boxes), Fruit Stripe, Adams' Sour Apple, Choward's Scented, Teaberry, Razzles (various flavors), Jolt, Double Bubble, a wide selection of bubble gum cigars and cigarettes, and those little gum "gold nuggets" that come in cotton bags tied with string. These are all up in the front of the store, which is heavily trafficked. I stood there staring at the Beeman's for a minute, thinking about Sven. I felt my eyes fill up with tears. I picked up three packs and ducked behind a rack of novelty items so nobody would see me cry. I wiped my eyes with the back of my hand and looked up at a giant Elvis Pez dispenser. They also had Darth Vader.

It took me a little while to collect myself.

When I left Economy Candy, I turned west on Ludlow, made a right on Delancey, and rounded the corner on Allen, where I ran straight into a pack of earnest young dancers swinging their arms up in assertive fifth positions *en haut*. The assertiveness of their dancing was all the more marked given the constraints of their garments: they were wearing trench coats! For a moment, I was sure they were a few members of the Performa crew who had gotten loose and were now roaming the city. But then I realized that their movement was altogether different. Except for their clothing, they bore no resemblance to the dancers I'd seen one week earlier.

There were a few curious on-lookers, some of whom appeared as befuddled as me. Others were calmly documenting the event on their cell phones. A straggly bunch of us hovered around the edges as the dancers lunged and leapt. Finally, they seemed to have reached their destination, and they emphatically tugged open their belts and ripped their jackets off, casting them to the ground in defiance.

That was when I noticed a sleek, slightly silvery figure darting around the corner out of sight – but I could swear – it looked just like Jimmy Stewart! He was also wearing a trench coat! He kept his on – obviously, he had something to hide!

The mystery was clarified, somewhat, in the Arts section of the *Times* on November 11. Gia Kourlas explained that a young choreographer of Turkish origins, Nejla Yatkin, had organized this dance as a celebration of the 20th anniversary of the fall of the Berlin wall. In her public statements about this piece, she said she wanted to remind people of the monumental nature of that event. As an Eastern European, she said, she felt she had a much more powerful sense of the oppressive history repre- sented by the wall. For her, the costuming was reminiscent of secret police, of a period of terrifying surveillance. The expres- sive movement of her dancers was intended to, in effect, break through the painful memories that their garments might evoke. Kourlas noted that that euphoric moment when they shed their coats might have been a tad too literal.

Of course none of this explained the apparition of that carper, the email jerk, on the Lower East Side that night. Was he just out stalking more dancers? Or was it something about this particular dance?

Was he stalking me?

And what was with the trench coat?

It occurred to me there were some fairly obvious reasons to wear a trench coat: because you were a detective, a spy, or a flasher. That is, because you had something to find, something to hide, or something you wanted desperately to show.

It was around this time that my advisor wrote me saying that she'd been contacted by the University of Malta. They were looking for an "emerging dance scholar" and she'd given them my name and an enthusiastic recommendation. This seemed like the only promising prospect on the horizon. That Academic Jobs Wiki was a daily source of mega downer updates on a grim grim situation.

Actually, a couple of people had posted that they'd already been contacted about those two long-shot stateside jobs I'd applied for. That didn't look too good for me.

I thought: "Really? The University of Malta? Is this my academic career?"

I wasn't thinking this exclusively with shock or chagrin. That is, there was some of that, but it also seemed a little bit like something that might happen in a dream.

In somewhat better news, though equally weird, I received an invitation from the famous performance artist, Vaginal Crème Davis, to assist her as a "choreographic dramaturg" on her performance in Bruce LaBruce's production of *The Bad Breast, or the Strange Case of Theda Lange* at the Brut Theater in Vienna. There seemed to be a grant involved, and Vag had approached José Muñoz about finding a dance dramaturg, and he indicated Lepecki of course, but André had other obligations at the time of the performance so he generously gave her my name and contact information.

She wrote me an email, but in peculiarly formal Victorian prose. It seemed like the kind of invitation that should have been written on embossed stationary, and indeed, she followed it with an actual letter scrawled around the edges of a photocopy of part of her face. The heading of her email was "I am Elijah Thrush," which I had to Google. Vag is very erudite. Anyway, the long and short of it was that through the Goethe Institute and some other unnamed resource (possibly related to LaBruce's porn industry connections), Vag was offering me a round-trip ticket to Vienna and five nights in some Kunsthaus dormitory situation to observe the performances of *The Bad*

Breast and offer some scholarly guidance regarding the choreography of object relations, and she added, "Darling Dr. Adams, all sources indicate that you would be a most stellar collaborator and I so hope you will grace us with your presence December 16 – 20 at the marvelous Brut Theater – isn't the name just delicious?"

She attached a link to the video of the film version of *The Bad Breast* that LaBruce had already made in Berlin. The response had been excellent, but as the stage version developed, they envisioned a more significant choreographic component, particularly for Vag's character. She wasn't explicitly referred to as "The Good Breast," although she did appear to be a sympathetic character. She was dressed in an enormous naked fat suit and inexplicably would tail the troubled female narrator around the streets of Berlin.

The timing was off: my lecture was scheduled for the 16th. But it struck me that if I could arrive a day late, then if I needed to make a quick escape in humiliation after my presentation this might be just the thing.

I had not made a lot of progress in preparing for my talk. In fact, none at all. I basically had no idea whatsoever about what I was going to say.

I wrote Vag that I'd be delighted to accept her invitation, but that I had a commitment on the 16th. She indicated that this would not be a problem as surely two or three viewings of *The Bad Breast* would give us plenty to discuss. Shortly thereafter I got an email in slightly stilted language from a staff member at the Goethe Institute confirming my itinerary. I was flying out bright and early on the morning of the 17th. I wasn't sure how qualified I was to dramaturg this piece, but the Academic Jobs Wiki indicated that if a person could add any professional credit to his or her CV, he or she had better do it. Besides, I kind of liked Vienna. And Vag seemed so nice to work with. I wondered if she had any interest in semaphore, or ballet positions. When I asked her, she answered, "Oh, Dr. Adams, I have the utmost respect for a truly dedicated scholar of the classical dance such as yourself, but I'm afraid everything I know I learned from the divine Kay Ambrose and her charming little volume THE BALLET-LOVER'S POCKET-BOOK."

Of course I immediately got on Amazon and ordered a used copy. The first edition was published in 1945. I found a 1972 edition for $6.00. When it arrived, I saw that even Miss Ambrose admitted that this was not a book for specialists such as myself. It was directed to the "thousands of Americans who have recently learned to love ballet." The author bio read:

> Kay Ambrose, brilliant English artist and balletomane, has illustrated many books, several of them written by herself. She has given exhibitions in England and Australia, has lectured on the theater and ballet at Oxford, Cambridge, Nottingham, and Reading universities, and has worked with Technicolor films. For the British Army Education Scheme she taught six-foot pupils from the Grenadier Guards and painted ballerinas on bombers and mermaids inside a French submarine. She has worked – and toured – with the National Ballet of Canada. Miss Ambrose was born and bred in Surrey. Her hobbies are cats, playing the guitar, sailing, and going to the theater. She visited the United States for the first time in 1948, and has returned often since then. Her small books on aspects of ballet have become standard throughout the English-speaking world.

Her drawings were very lively – they showed not only positions and physical maneuvers, but also costumes and cosmetic effects. In the opening set of sketches, she shows the make-up tricks for Pétrouchka ("a doll's face painted by an absent-minded crafts-man – yet he must be tragic – not comic or grotesque!"), the greasy "Dago" from *Façade*, the Chinese maiden from *L'Épreuve d'Amour*, and the "Faune" of the famous *après-midi*.

Of course I already owned the classic coffee table book of ballet technique, Kirstein, Stuart and Dyer's *The Classic Ballet: Basic Technique and Terminology*, and I had any number of aca-demic tomes on the history of classical dance, from the stodgy to the poststructural, but I must confess I found Miss Ambrose's text, with its catty little references to the behind-the-scenes she-nanigans of dancers, oddly captivating. And because it was a "pocket-book," it was very easy to carry around.

I started to carry it around.

How did the next five weeks pass? In an inexplicable blur. My daily routine was consistent (breakfast reading the *Times*, *barre* exercises, some comma excisions and replacements, lunch, an outing to the gym, a shower, a trip to the library to check on a reference or photocopy a bibliography, a quick chat with Dan, Fang, or Ellen, an occasional beer or film or performance event, a text or email to Sven, maybe a little sudoku to make myself sleepy, and lights out. Sometimes I'd flirt a little in a bar. To be honest, once I had slightly desultory hand sex with a guy I met. More typically, I managed to take care of myself. Once in a while I'd jot down some notes about possible plot devices for the novel I was thinking of writing. I was keeping them in a file. Periodically I'd have a panic attack, with visions of the moth, the carper, and a sea of beige, belted drones.

And then it was December 15.

I was, as the colorful expression goes, up shit creek without a paddle.

Ramon had posted the announcement for my talk on the departmental list-serve, and at my request had just put the title of my dissertation and the short abstract, as I figured I'd be pulling something from that. But as I stared at the bloated chapters, bottom-heavy with their rambling endnotes, I knew I couldn't go through with it.

That's when I clicked on YouTube.

On December 16, I arrived in the department 15 minutes before my talk. Ramon asked me if I needed help setting anything up. I said no, thanks – I was just going to screen a couple of YouTube videos. He said, "Okay, Gray, you da man!" He meant this in a friendly, joking way. He seemed to believe, however, that I could pull this off. Why? I prepared the video links on the projection screen and shuffled my papers at the lectern. People started to filter in. Fang and Dan, of course, were there early. They gave me smiles of encouragement. Several eager-beaver MA students, who were gung-ho about nearly everything, took their seats toward the front. To my surprise, a few faculty members actually showed up. Schechner was there. He was already sketching in his notebook. I thought I also recognized Mark Franko, the famous dance scholar. Talk about pressure. Franko had recently taken over the editorial reins at *Dance Research Journal*. I wondered if I was going to make it through this. Just a minute or so before I was scheduled to start talking, both Muñoz and Lepecki slipped in. I overheard them deferentially offering to let each other introduce me. Muñoz got the hot potato, I guess, because as the clock ticked in at 5:05 p.m. he gently came over to me and whispered, "I'm going to do a quick introduction." Lepecki slipped into the seat beside Franko.

I stepped a bit to the side to make room for Muñoz at the podium. He leaned over it and read from the boilerplate bio I'd given to Ramon in preparation for this day. My heart was starting to thud distractingly, but I was able to follow, barely, the brief account of my artistic and scholarly training and the reiteration of the short abstract of my dissertation that everybody had presumably already read on the list-serve, at which point he looked up from his script to add, "which, I believe, will be the basis of his talk today. Please join me in welcoming our distinguished visiting scholar, Gray Adams."

The twenty-odd people in the room clapped politely.

I cleared my throat and said, "Actually, I have a new title for this talk. It's called: 'Stalkers, Spies and Flashers.'" I thought I sensed a pricking up of certain ears in the room. Out of the corner of my eye I saw Schechner making some hatch marks on his sketch.

I began, "November 1, 2009 was the opening ceremony of Performa 2009, the biennial performance art festival run by RoseLee Goldberg. The festivities were supposed to start at 8 p.m. in Times Square. Arto Lindsay, the sound artist, had collaborated with the choreographer Lily Baldwin on a kind of parade."

I clicked on the video, which streamed behind me as I continued. I narrated the set-up, the execution, and the after-effects of what I'd seen. I gave a brief summary of the history of the "flash mob," and the ways in which it demonstrated from its inception the complicated relationship between anarchy, choreographed spontaneity, and commercialism. Of this particular performance, I said, "It may have had indeterminate political *goals*, but it certainly did feel representative of the political and aesthetic moment, one that Lauren Berlant has characterized as 'a space of abeyance.'" I'd found this essay by Berlant the night before, Googling "the politics of lurking." Need I say, I was thinking not only about this choreography, but also myself. I continued: "In the desire expressed by various political factions for 'less filter,' Berlant notes a yearning for a certain kind of intimate public sphere. An intimate public, she says, 'promises the sense of being loosely held in a social world.'" Here I quoted Silvan Tomkins about how you might enjoy a particular kind of embrace... Perhaps a loose one, rendered by a social world... I returned to Berlant: "'You don't have to do anything to belong, once you show up and listen. You can be passive and lurk in an intimate public.' Lurking, Berlant tells us, means our communications are increasingly constituted by what we overhear. Ambient sound, she says, engenders 'ambient citizenship.'"

I went on to describe Yatkin's choreography, and projected images of her belted, dronish dancers pirouetting through the Lower East Side. I tried, vaguely, to parse out the differences between the ambiguous anti-commercialism of the Performa pseudo-flash mob and the equally confusing anti-Communism of Nejla Yatkin's self-disrobing secret police. I said something about sentiment, and nostalgia for a time of political and economic clarity. And I considered the trench coat.

I said, "There are three reasons to wear a trench coat: because you have something to find, something to hide, or something you want desperately to show. The garment that seems to beg you, 'Don't notice me!' is also begging you to take notice, whether the wearer wants you to see what's underneath, or whether he wants you simply to fear it. But part of the contract is for the wearer and the witness – who is also being watched – to maintain the fiction of the non-theatricality, of the non-spectacularity, of the extreme understatement of the performance."

As I said this, my mind shot to the image of Jimmy Stewart scurrying around the corner in all his beige minimalism.

I concluded somewhat lyrically: "We increasingly move through a soundscape both *overheard* and *understated*. It emanates from the earbuds of the iPods and cell phones of our fellow passengers, who may or may not be fellow travelers – or perhaps they're indicating to us what it means now, maybe always meant, to be a fellow traveler, an unacknowledged intimate in a political sphere that attempts to cover itself in discretion even as it exposes itself."

There was a beat.

Then Fang, unable to contain herself, said, "This is, after all, how ideology works."

I stared back at her. There was an awkward pause, and then I looked up and said, "That's it." People clapped. Actually, they clapped quite enthusiastically. It was a big relief. I'd nearly filled my allotted time slot. The party was about to begin.

José Muñoz stood and faced the audience and said, "Great, umm, I think we have time for maybe one question or so – and we hope of course you'll all stick around for our holiday party which starts in just a few minutes up on the 12th floor in the Dean's Conference Room. Any questions? Comments?"

Another brief, awkward pause. I think people had liked the talk, but it was the end of the semester, they were tired, and they were all thinking about the holiday punch and other refreshments awaiting them upstairs – so Dan Ferguson just tossed out a fake, jokey pseudo-question to give us an excuse to break: "Okay then, Gray, what about you? Do you have something to find, something to hide, or something you want desperately to show?"

Everyone laughed nervously, and I said, "I'm not sure."

The holiday party was great. I don't know if it was Ramon's famous coconut punch or if it was the relief of having made it through my talk, but I got smashed pretty quickly. There was some greasy fried food and there were some retro baked goods that students, staff, and faculty members had entered in a competition. There was a pineapple upside-down cake, several items involving marshmallow fluff, and a spiked Jell-O fruit mold.

There was a disco ball and a karaoke machine, and before

long people were crooning embarrassingly to "Don't Cry for Me, Argentina." When the dancing started, I worried somebody was going to get hurt. Some people were very expressive movers.

I saw a guy I'd been meaning to speak with. He was a Greek PhD student who wrote about experimental sound. His particular area of expertise was the electric guitar. He had black-rimmed glasses and a tidy goatee. He was small and compact, concentrated, and vital. His name was Stefanos. While I'd seen him making many acute theoretical comments at academic talks, he was quite the wild man on the dance floor. After a while he took a break to get another glass of punch. He wiped the sweat from his brow as he stood in line. He was next to a beautiful blonde woman who stood several inches taller than him. I walked over to say hello, and he looked up and said with great warmth, "Gray, have you met my lover?" He gently put his arm around the blonde woman. She politely extended her hand so I could shake it. You might say her bearing was regal. In a nice way.

I meant to ask him if he could give me any bibliographic leads on the electric guitar, since this was an increasing preoccupation of mine. But I was so taken aback by how gentlemanly he seemed that night, and how beautiful his "lover" was, I didn't ask him. I was also, as I mentioned, drunk.

Later Stefanos sang a karaoke version of "Bohemian Rhapsody." He also wiped out spinning a girl around on roller-blades and got a little blood on his shirt but just kept dancing.

The morning of the 17th I had a bad headache, but I managed to make it to JFK in time for my flight. Sven and I thought for a minute about meeting in Vienna, but I already had my ticket to go to Stockholm in January and besides I thought I'd be busy working on *The Bad Breast*. And it's true, as soon as I got there I threw my bag in the austere dorm room and Vag's friend Ilhan took me over to the Brut Theater.

For the next three days, it was a pretty constant barrage of fake flesh, obscure psychoanalytic references and mild porn, genial conversations over schnapps, and animated exchanges of enthusiasm for "the divine Kay Ambrose" between myself and Vag. I actually thought the production didn't need too much choreography on top of Vag's commanding performance. It's what you might call "gilding the lily." But we did work out some subtle modifications of her hand gestures.

On the night of the last performance, the cast wanted to go out after the show to a bar called Alte Lampe. This place was known as a meeting place for the Wiener Runde (bears). But for some reason I was feeling mildly melancholy and so I claimed to have a migraine and went back to the dorm room. I texted Sven (*"jag saknar dig"* – miss you), checked my email (the University of Malta was requesting a writing sample), and clicked on YouTube. I just wanted to see if anything had happened over on Nethermost's page.

No action, so far as I could tell. That last post had gotten a few more hits, but no more comments. I looked in the column of related videos – there were a few other psychedelic versions of classical compositions. One looked interesting: Edvard Grieg's *In der Halle des Bergkönigs* played by Big Brother and the Holding Company. I clicked on it – it was great. The footage was black and white, from a television broadcast in 1967. There was a brief interview beforehand, and then an extended, bizarre, and virtuosic interpretation.

And then I saw it: the topmost comment, freshly sent by "hmmbcker52": "SAINT JAMES, 12/22/1939 – 12/20/2009: R.I.P." My God. James Gurley was dead.

WHY YURI GAGARIN?

I was in Vienna the day that James Gurley died.

How did I not see it coming? The line about the "GURLY BOY"… Gurley's vaguely disappointing performance in Woodstock with that Japanese pop star had perhaps made it difficult for me to see, but now it all made sense. And just because I'd solved the mystery of James Gurley didn't mean I wasn't also implicated – me, and others like me… I saw again the ominous glower of John Wayne in that shop window, hailing me as his "KITCHEN BITCH"…

My mind was racing… There were so many dots to connect… Gurley had clearly been some kind of visionary, seeing the classical potential within the uniquely expressive distortion guitar. He'd been onto this since 1967, at least. Could it have been Gurley playing on the moth's psychedelia vids?

And then an even more terrifying thought came to me: WAS GURLEY THE CAB FRESHENER ON TYPOS?! Was that the "secret"?!

These thoughts preoccupied me through my flight back to New York. I kept going back over the clues, but there was so much missing information. Where was Gurley when he died, and what were the circumstances? Where was Jimmy Stewart? My own last sighting placed him in New York November 8th, but he could have relocated since then. I wondered if Galina might spill any beans on his recent activities.

I took the AirTrain to the C and emerged from the West 4th Street station as the sun was making its seasonally appropriate but drearily early descent. When I got to my building, Jorge opened the door for me saying, "Good afternoon, sir, how are you?" I noticed Bugs Bunny's sister was sitting in one of the chairs in the lobby, dressed in her winter coat, her walker parked by her side. She seemed to be just hanging out.

I said, "HOW ARE YOU?"

She said, "WHAT? I CYAN HEAH YA!"

I repeated myself and she said, "AW, I'M DOIN' OKAY, TANKS. BUT IT'S COLD! I WISH I WAS IN MIAMI, I LOVE MIAMI! I TINK I NEED A NEW SCAWF. MAKE SHUAH YA WEAH A SCAWF!"

I promised I would.

When I got up to my place, I unpacked, watered the plants (deer looked okay), took a quick shower, fixed myself some tea and a plate of graham crackers, and sat down to Google "james gurley circumstances of death december 20 2009." Unfortunately, the terms "circumstances of death december 20 2009" called up an enormous number of items relating to the untimely demise of Brittany Murphy, a beautiful, young actress. The overwhelming public interest in her story outweighed the specificity of my inputting "james gurley," so I had to sift through a few pages before I actually got anything I was looking for.

Brittany Murphy, by the way, appeared to have died of natural causes – or at least, there appeared to be no foul play, though a depressing history of eating disorders might have contributed to other pre-existing health problems.

Of course, James Gurley also appeared to have died of

natural causes. And at his age, after a famously hard-rocking life, nobody seemed particularly surprised. I was the only one who was freaking out. But plenty of other people were sad to see him go.

"Saint James" was a nickname Gurley had applied to himself, but lots of fans were happy to adopt it in reference to him. Sainthood was not the only figure they invoked. He was also hailed as an astronaut – actually, a cosmonaut. Country Joe & the Fish's guitarist, Barry Melton, said, "James Gurley was the first man in space! He's the Yuri Gagarin of psychedelic guitar." That was quoted in pretty much every obituary I found. I found it interesting Melton had compared him to a Soviet space hero. Surely he could have called him "the first guitarist on the moon" – the Neil Armstrong of the electric guitar.

When I'd skimmed over all the Gurley obituaries, I checked in on Nethermost's page. No new comments. That could be either good or bad news.

That reference to Gagarin made me think of Galina. The obituaries hadn't turned up a lot of dirt on Gurley's end, but maybe if I approached it from Jimmy Stewart's… It was time for another reconnaissance mission at the Torch Club.

One minor problem. Cash flow. My ticket to Vienna and that dorm room had been covered, of course, but the incidentals – chipping in to cover the tab for Wiener Schnitzels and schnapps – had done a number on my already piddly stash. There were still nine days to get through in the month of December. I resolved to subsist on rice and Goya beans, and to bank one final holiday *tarte tatin* with some Earl Grey tea at my gentlemen's club before it shut down for the NYU winter break.

After all, I told myself, it was in the name of research. And not just academic research. This might be a matter of life and death.

When I got to the club, I saw that they'd put up the even-handed assortment of "holiday" decorations that maintained the appropriate balance between Judeo and Christian influences, avoiding the most tacky of Pagan ones. Galina, however, was unapologetically sporting a glittery red sweater with a Christmas tree on it. She tried to push the pumpkin pie on me, but I held fast to my plan. "I'll have the *tarte tatin*, please, and a pot of Earl Grey."

Then, as nonchalantly as I could, I said, "By the way, have you seen that gentleman recently? Did you say he played racquet sports at Duke? I think I might have accidentally picked up his umbrella the last time we were both here." I indicated a little fus-chia compact umbrella with a Duane Reade insignia I'd brought along as part of my ruse. I was hoping she wouldn't remember it hadn't been raining that day.

She looked suspiciously at my prop. "This is not umbrella of sportsman." I think she might have found this cheap drugstore item a slight to his signature style. Or maybe it was the color. She said, "He is more rugged type guy. He visits mother in state Vermont! And you are going to see mother for kholidays?"

No, I wasn't going to visit my mother for the holidays, I hadn't for some time, and she'd certainly managed to hit the old nail of guilt on the head with that one. I wasn't even going to spend Christmas with my boyfriend, or, as Stefanos might have put it, my lover. I'd just gotten back from hanging out in Vienna with some avant-garde pornographers, and I was going to plow right through the next several days combing the Internet for any trace of incriminating evidence against JIMMY STEWART, for God's sake, friend to giant talking bunnies and America's sweet-heart, who at this very moment was probably home chopping firewood for his adorable old pie-baking mom. What was wrong with this picture? Besides the unconvincing subterfuge of my fuschia umbrella?

One thing made me feel a little better. One person, that is. When I got back to my building, Bugs Bunny's sister was again sitting in the lobby. She saw me and hollered, "AW GEE, DAT'S SUCH A PWETTY UMBWELLA. I JUS' LOVE DAT CULLAH, WHAT IS DAT, HOT PINK?"

I said, "PLEASE, TAKE IT, IT'S YOURS."

She said, "YAW GIVIN' DAT TA ME? YAW SUCH A NICE POYSON. TANKS SO MUCH."

Bugs Bunny's sister surely wouldn't think it was weird I had no plans for Christmas. She was Jewish.

When I got upstairs I texted Sven that I knew an old lady who could use a scarf, if he felt like knitting one. He liked to receive knitting assignments. It gave him a goal. He texted back, "*inga problem* :-)" He'd have it ready when I went to visit him in two weeks.

I didn't mention James Gurley – and I certainly didn't mention Brittany Murphy. That would really have gotten him down.

My on-the-ground sleuthing had only rendered this: that Jimmy Stewart was a better son than I was, and right now he appeared to be living the "rugged" filial life in Vermont. But could I trust information coming from Galina? They were very friendly. Also, she seemed easily buffaloed.

I couldn't keep obsessing about this 24/7. As had been the case with each of my prior panics, the Gurley demise was beginning to look quite possibly innocent. It was really only when I considered the accumulation of weird coincidences that my heart would start pounding, only to settle again when I went back over the rational explanations.

Meanwhile, I had to figure out what writing sample to send

the University of Malta. The obvious thing would have been the introduction of my manuscript, along with the abstract. On the other hand, the response had been surprisingly positive to my talk in the department. In fact, Richard Schechner had even approached me at the holiday party about publishing a version in *TDR*, the prestigious performance journal he edited. At first I thought he was just drunk like me, or being collegial, but maybe there was something of interest in my paranoid ramblings.

You have probably surmised: with the exception of those quotes from Lauren Berlant, I basically pilfered the whole talk from the notes I'd been making for that novel I was thinking of writing.

I sent the text of my talk to Schechner, and to Malta.

Christmas was a little lonely. Fang and Dan were with their respective families. Ellen had gone to stay with her mother for a while in Minnesota. She took her cat. Randy and Jeremy were at Randy's brother's place in Ohio. Sven texted me from his parents' place in Malmö. He said, "*det snöar.*" It's snowing.

I'd ordered *Laura* from Netflix. Dan had told me about it. He said, "Vincent Price plays the love interest. He's actually supposed to be hot, and the weird thing is, he kind of is. He has a Southern accent about a third of the time."

It was strange, all right, to see Vincent Price play the Southern stud. But to me, stranger still was Dana Andrews in that trench coat! Naturally, he was the one I identified with. He's Mark McPherson, the hard-boiled detective they put on the Laura Hunt murder case. There's a series of suspicious characters – Laura's controlling professional mentor, her homely maiden aunt, Price as a freeloading Southern gentleman who wants to marry her, and Laura's totally crushed-out lesbian maid. Each one of them gives the detective bits of information about the dead woman, and their stories are illustrated in flashback scenes which, I suppose, are filmic representations of the detective's imagination as he hears these stories. It also helps that there's a huge painted portrait of Laura in her apartment.

Between staring at that portrait and hearing from everybody about how captivating she was, Mark McPherson slowly finds himself falling in love with Laura. There's just one problem: she's dead. Waldo, that controlling mentor, says, "You better watch out, McPherson, or you'll end up in a psychiatric ward. I don't think they've ever had a patient who fell in love with a corpse." McPherson tries to act cool, but you can see that comment throws him for a loop.

Then – surprise – it turns out she's not dead! She comes home from a long weekend in the country to discover Mark McPherson poking around all her personal effects in her living room. She's of course miffed at first, but then he explains there's been a murder. It turns out it was some model who just happened to be lounging around Laura's house dressed in one of her negligees. Somebody must have knocked her off thinking she was Laura. Once they figure this out, there seems to be a little romantic spark between Laura and McPherson, though she briefly appears to be tempted to go back to Vincent Price.

The incipient romance with McPherson infuriates Waldo, who's had a hard enough time convincing Laura that Vincent Price was a cad. Now he has to talk her down from falling for the detective. Waldo tells her, "When you were unattainable, when he thought you were dead, that's when he wanted you most."

I won't give away the end, but suffice it to say, you really can't trust Waldo.

Still, I found his observations pretty acute. And profoundly disturbing.

He may actually have a point. Why *would* a man be particularly attracted to somebody who was already dead? I could think of several reasons, and they all made me sad.

Waldo has most of the good lines in this film. At one point he says, "Laura dear, I cannot stand these morons any longer. If you do not come with me this instant I shall run amok."

My New Year's Eve was slightly livelier than my Christmas. Fang was back, and she called to tell me José Muñoz was having a little get-together at his place. I thought it would probably be mostly faculty and some of his artist friends, but Fang was invited because she sometimes walked Muñoz's dog. She was sure it would be okay if I went along. I thought my new association with Vag maybe also put me in a special category. I got kind of dressed up. It's not that I was so excited – I was actually feeling a little anti-social – but it wasn't often I had an excuse to get out my nice clothes. I wore an old smoking jacket I had. When I went to get the elevator, I saw Bugs Bunny's sister inching her way down the hallway with her walker. She was wearing a sequined pink sweatshirt depicting fireworks and she had on red lipstick.

She looked terrific.

She screamed, "WATCHA DOIN' FA NEW YEAH'S?"

I said, "PARTY!"

She said, "AW DAT'S GWEAT! YA LOOK SO HAN'SOME. I'M GOIN' TA ENNIO'S! DEY GOTTA SPECIAL, YA GET A GLASS O' CHAMPAGNE WIT YA SPAGHETTI!"

I smiled and nodded.

She said, "I'M TELLIN' YA, I HAD A GWEAT LIFE, I BEEN TA ALL DA BES' SPOTS, I USE'TA GO TA DA GWEAT WESOAHTS, YA KNOW, DA STAHDUST, DA DEAUVILLE, I SAW DA SHOWS AT ALL DA BES' CLUBS, IT WAS GWEAT. BUT NOW, YA KNOW WHAT I WEALLY

LIKE TA DO? I HAVE A LITTLE GLASS O' CHAMPAGNE AN' I GO BACK HOME AN' WATCH DA BALL DWOP ON DA TELEVISION. I LIKE DAT. I LIKE TO WATCH IT ON DA TELEVISION, AN' DEN I GO TA BED."

That actually sounded like a good idea, but I'd told Fang I'd meet her in the lobby of Muñoz's building. I didn't want to disappoint her.

When I got there, Fang was holding a tray of deviled eggs. I'd thought I should really have something to offer myself but somehow didn't think my rice and Goya beans were going to make much of an impression, so I hitched a free ride on Fang's hors d'oeuvres.

It was pretty lively up there. Carmelita Tropicana was passing out little party hats and tooty horns. A couple of people had brought their dogs in full festive regalia. Nao Bustamante's toy poodle had little reindeer antlers – I guess these were left over from Christmas. Dulce Maria was wearing a rhinestone collar and a tutu. That, naturally, affected me.

There was an attractive blonde woman of a certain age holding court in the corner, and Fang whispered to me that she was the former Warhol star, Bibbe Hansen. She said she was also Beck's mother.

Muñoz came over to me at one point and told me he'd liked my talk. He asked me if I had any plans after my fellowship was finished. I told him I was up for a job in Malta.

He said, "Did you say 'in the mountains'?" The music was kind of loud.

I said, "No, Malta."

He just looked at me.

Fang was squatting on the floor, scratching Dulce's belly. She seemed to be in heaven. Dulce, I mean.

The next week I flew to Stockholm. The January trip was always the hard one. It's not the cold that gets to you so much, it's the shortness of the days. The whole time I was living there, I never got used to it. Sven, of course, didn't know anything different. He was a little glum these days, but it wasn't really about the darkness.

That first evening we stayed in and cooked together. We made pasta and had a little red wine. We listened to Johnny Mathis.

I like Johnny Mathis. My mother liked Johnny Mathis when I was a kid.

My time in Stockholm was pretty mellow. As his doctor had predicted, Sven seemed to be adjusting to his meds. The dreams were still a problem, but his stomach wasn't bothering him so much. His doctor was still encouraging him to try that FOTO regimen, but he wasn't quite ready to give it a go. His numbers were good.

That week Sven was pretty busy at the museum. They were preparing an exhibit of lacquer works by Nagatoshi Onishi. Sven was helping organize the installation. I went in with him one day, and while he was helping the curator figure out the placement of some of the pieces, I hung out in his office and wasted some time on his computer. You'll never guess where I ended up: back on Nethermost's channel. I'd been making a conscious effort not to obsess about her and the cab freshener, once I'd convinced myself that my panic over the Gurley incident was exaggerated. But I must confess it was an immense relief to see that she'd posted a new video, and that the freshener had already responded.

It was a solo again – this time to a sort of peculiar tune called, apparently, *Elephant* (the reason for this was not clear). It was in an unusual and irregular time signature, with a pounding bass drum below a rather tender and lyrical tenor voice. I believe I already mentioned – I have a penchant for unusual time signatures. The words were evocative but obscure – something about a "muddy arm... I wonder, I wonder what everyone is doing at home... the skin on my tree is growing back again... I'll move a little foot to the right, oh heavenly..." And being a literalist, the moth moved a little foot to the right.

Since the line was repeated several times, she eventually nudged herself entirely out of the picture. The rest of her movement phrases seemed, as in her prior choreographies, to be based on some weird grammar. I thought, for some reason, of the first chapter of Mark Franko's book, *Dance as Text*, in which he recounts the birth of theatrical dance in France. He says that a particular genre of baroque dance – "geometrical" choreography – was contrived to present the body of the dancer as a written text. These dances used "figures" – static or directional patterns – which were metaphors for writing on the page.

In reading these patterns, Franko quotes Pascal's *Pensées*: "*Figure porte absence et presence, plaisir et déplaisir.*" The figure brings absence and presence, pleasure and displeasure.

This was precisely my experience in watching this video.

I couldn't really say what was going on tonally in this piece. Both the music and the dance hovered in a space I'd call, for lack of a better term, irresolute. Or rather, it seemed almost like she was being intentionally misleading.

There was one decisive element: a new representational painting on the wall depicting an ominous, actually terrifying, male figure in a cowboy hat and an eye patch. The background was black. In fact, not just black, but blacker than black. It seemed to suck the light out of the room. I think it may have been black velvet. The ominous cowboy's one good eye seemed to be trained on the moth throughout her dance.

The email jerk had been the first to weigh in: "i luv it!!! bout time u put up 'A CERTN PRSN'..."

The cab freshener said, "I loved a certain person ardently and my love was not return'd..."

To which Nethermost answered (reassuringly? mockingly?), "'Why do I love' You, Sire?"

And then somebody called "BogusRetroCorn" wrote: "I can tell you why I love her. I have a lust for her dignity... I think of wonderful, exciting, decent things when I look at her..."

This really gave me pause. I thought it was maybe the sexiest and most gentlemanly thing I'd ever heard, with the possible exception of the way that guy Stefanos had introduced me to his girlfriend. But for some reason, I also found it vaguely menacing. Depending on how you read it, the conflation of "lust" and "decency" could either open up all kinds of possibilities – or shut them down.

And then, as if to confirm my discomfort, he added: "Get off your butt and join the Marines!"

omg. It was him. The elephant in the room.

The Duke.

A couple of days later I was hanging out at Sven's while he was at work. I did some *barre* exercises (always frustrating at his place, which was kind of cramped), took a quick shower, and decided to walk around the neighborhood even though it was already dark. I headed down Katarina Bangata. I walked by a little café we sometimes went to called Twang. They had a great vegetarian pâté, and excellent coffee. But I was a little low on cash so I just looked in the window.

As the name implied, this was a theme café. There were guitars suspended from the walls, and in the window, a lot of ukes. They were just hanging there, innocently, in the window. They struck, as it were, a chord.

I rushed back to Sven's to check in on the moth.

As I mentioned, my response to that BogusRetroCorn comment on her dance was one of ambivalence. But the cab freshener *really* didn't take it so well. In fact, he seemed to be reading it as a threat to the moth. He'd written two comments in rapid succession: "democracy… ma femme…" and then, "I think I could not refuse this moment to die for you, if that would save you."

BogusRetroCorn snapped back: "Every time you turn around expect to see me. 'Cause one time you'll turn around and I'll be there."

Oh God. Maybe this *was* serious.

When Sven got home I had to pretend everything was normal, but I was itching to get back to New York.

When I got back to my sublet, I unpacked. The first thing I pulled out of my suitcase was the scarf Sven had knit for Bugs Bunny's sister. It was made out of an off-white yarn with little flecks of other colors in it. I thought it would go nicely with her winter coat, which was also off-white. This set off her tan, which she seemed to maintain in the winter months by sitting outside as often as was possible. Even on chilly days, if the sun was out, she'd sometimes sit in it.

I went down the hall with the scarf. I heard the television on in her apartment. She was watching Jeopardy and the volume was up very loud. I was pretty sure she wouldn't hear me if I knocked, so I went back to my place and found one of those paper gift bags stored in a closet. The bag was silver and had an unused gift card attached to it. I wrote a note on the card. I said, "From your neighbor, Gray (15E)." I hesitated for a second, and then I wrote my phone number and said, "Call if you need anything." I left the bag with the scarf and the note outside her door.

That was about 7 p.m. I straightened up a bit, showered, heated up some soup, and when I couldn't stand it any longer I checked in again on the moth's channel. No action whatsoever. I watched the confusing dance one more time, scrolled through the list of related videos (largely elephant-themed), and then gave up for the night. I was shutting down my computer when I thought I heard a tap at the door. When I opened it, it was Bugs Bunny's sister. She was wearing the scarf, and she had the gift bag in her hand. She wagged the bag at me and said, "DIDJOO PUT DIS IN FWONT O' MY DOAH? I WAS PUTTIN' DA GAHBAGE OUT AN' I ALMOS' FELL OVAH DIS."

I said, "SORRY, YES."

I was a little worried she might be mad at me, but she said, "DAT IS SO NICE. TANKS VEWY MUCH. YAW A WEAL NICE FELLA, I'M TELLIN' YA. I WASN'T SO SHUAH AT FOYST." She winked.

I said, "MY FRIEND MADE IT. I HOPE YOU LIKE IT."

She said, "IT'S BYOOFUL, I LOVE IT, BUT HEAH, TAKE YA BAG BACK SO YA CAN USE IT AGAIN, IT'S STILL GOOD."

I looked at the silver bag. Indeed, there was nothing wrong with it.

I said, "OKAY, BUT HERE, KEEP THE CARD, IT'S GOT MY NUMBER IN CASE OF AN EMERGENCY."

She looked very closely at the card and said, "IS DIS YAW NUMBAH? OH, I'M GONNA NEED DAT. OKAY. GIMME JUST DA CAWD."

I carefully detached it without tearing the number. She looked at it closely again and repeated, "I'M GONNA NEED DAT."

This made me feel simultaneously flattered and a little afraid. That one time I'd tried to help her with the Access-A-Ride number I hadn't really accomplished anything. Still, if I *could* be of help, I thought I'd like to. We both smiled a kind of wan smile and nodded at each other, and she inched her way back home with her walker. I watched her until she made it in her door, and I went back into my apartment.

I was pretty tired because of the time difference in Sweden, and because of the journey, which, even when it went smoothly, was fairly grueling.

I went to bed. I imagine Bugs Bunny's sister did, too.

D.O.A.

*S*ven texted me, "omg watch d.o.a. :O "

I put *D.O.A.* at the top of my Netflix queue and it arrived two days later. Indeed. omg. :O

It's the story of some small-town notary public who can't quite bring himself to commit to his very nice but clingy girlfriend. He decides to take a little trip on his own for the weekend and ends up surrounded by a bunch of drunk conventioneers. He flirts a little and ties one on, but nothing extreme. But the next morning he wakes up feeling terrible. It's worse than a garden-variety hangover. He goes to a doctor and lo and behold, the doctor gives him some shockingly bad news: he's been poisoned! He has a "luminous toxin" in his system for which there's no antidote: he'll be dead in a couple of days!

At first he refuses to believe it. There's no reason for anybody to want him dead. Those drunken conventioneers were buffoons, but not cold-blooded murderers. He figures he doesn't just have a couple of days to live – he's got a couple of days to figure out who the hell would want him dead.

The girlfriend, who also happens to be his office manager, is dragged through a series of partial revelations that confuse, hurt, and confound her, but she's determined to stand by her man. She really wants to get married.

His fearlessness (what has he got left to lose?) and her

investigative pluck finally expose the reason behind his poisoning. It's entirely banal. There was some plot involving Eastern European gangsters, an import/export operation, some stolen iridium, a devious accountant, and a couple of illicit love affairs. None of this involved the notary. It was just his bad luck that one of these gangsters had him notarize the bill of sale on his iridium. The notary's ledger had a record of the transaction, and the only way the schemers could cover their trail was to off said notary.

In other words, the guy got himself killed for a very chump-change reason: for being a small-town, sad-ass notary public.

Even with the academic job market in ruins, I don't think I could bring myself to work as a notary public. Though that Academic Jobs Wiki would have you believe that when all you've got going for you is a PhD in the humanities and a former life as a ballet dancer, you might very well want to explore this kind of career option.

I spent the next couple of weeks piddling away my time. It dawned on me that my post-doctoral fellowship was now more than half over. It was to be disbursed over one calendar year, which had begun in September. We were barreling toward the end of January, and I had only accomplished the title change and a bit of comma fudging. I did write that talk on trench coats, but as I mentioned, that wasn't even intended to be an academic paper. I was just gathering material for that novel I'd been thinking about writing. For obvious reasons, I'd been considering the murder mystery as a genre.

As I scrolled through my manuscript – my academic manuscript – I found myself fixating on certain passages – the description of Noverre's *Jason et Médée* with its pantomimic representations of the motive and weapons of murder (Jealousy,

Fire, Steel) – the passage from *Die Welt des Tänzers* about the ecstasies of terror and hatred, joy and desire – that gruesome account of Forsythe's dancers dismembered by frustrated passion…

There was something from *Decreation* that flashed into my head – something about secrets and lies… All these moments in which the attempt to communicate something through gesture led to inevitable violence. I remembered that video of the moth's, the first psychedelic *Gnossienne*. I opened my browser and went to her channel. I clicked on "lent (2) satie."

I couldn't believe what I saw. A slew of new comments had turned up – and recently. There was a breathless exchange between the moth and the cab freshener, and its apparent urgency had me at the edge of my seat.

A week before, she had written, confusingly: "Better of it – continual be afraid – Than it – And Whom you told it to – beside – " It seemed to me a desperate warning. Her peculiar syntax could only indicate utter panic.

And yet he wrote back, with apparent tranquility: "Dear friend whoever you are take this kiss."

Whoever you are?

There was a pause of a couple of days, and then she added: "Going to Heaven! I don't know when – " and then: "If you should get there first Save just a little space for me"

To which he answered (reassuringly? alarmingly?): "Be it as if I were with you (Be not too certain but I am now with you.)"

The email jerk butted in: "@AhNethermostFun: As for you an me an our mistical connect. Two pees in a pod babe. Two pees in a pod."

From Nethermost: no comment.

From ACabFreshenerOnTypos, defiantly: "We are those two natural and nonchalant persons."

And then finally, the very day of my helpless witnessing of these communications, Nethermost blurted two horrific, urgent, hysterical comments that made my heart stop: "Murder by degrees – A Thrust – and then for Life a chance – " and then: "Had I a mighty gun I think I'd shoot the human race."

Which prompted from the cab freshener, devastatingly: "It appears to me I am dying… I love you… I am as one disembodied, triumphant, dead."

They were freaking me out!

I copied and pasted the string of comments into a Word document, and then began scanning over the various other comment strings on the moth's first and second channels, reversing their order to reconstruct the sequence of their appearance. I went back over the other videos that had sparked my interest – the moonwalker in Belarus, Makarova, Lutz Forster, Merce, that Les Paul documentary – collecting every vaguely pertinent quip that might give a clue as to the email jerk's next move. I combed through my file of trench coat documents, pulling other details that might add up to something. I even pulled the ominous passages from my academic manuscript – anything to help me figure out where this was headed. I shuffled them around, trying to make sense of the timeline. I jotted notes between them, attempting to find some continuity, some sensible plot.

I realized some of the connections were tenuous at best. Even if I were to hand this material over to the authorities, I was pretty sure they'd shrug it off as the product of my overactive imagination. But I couldn't shake my suspicion anymore: Jimmy Stewart was up to no good. Whether he was acting on his own or under the sway of that creepy sidekick of his, "the Duke," the moth was in danger, and so was her liberal friend the freshener.

I printed the whole file of evidence. It must have weighed a pound.

I took a blank piece of paper and sketched a rough graph of connections between discrete events and persons, noting the dates of particularly menacing appearances or utterances by the jerk.

I looked around for a binder or folder to put these materials in, but the only thing I could find was that sparkly silver gift bag returned to me by Bugs Bunny's sister. I put the stack of print-outs into the bag.

I'd worked myself into something of a tizzy. I needed to find the jerk. I didn't know what I'd say to him if I found him, but I knew I had to do something. But where to find him? My last visit to my gentlemen's club had been a total bust.

Then I remembered the NYU gym. I hadn't been there in a while. I'd really been slacking off on my cardio workout, although I'd been fairly diligent about the *barre* exercises. At that moment, I really didn't need to get my heart rate *up* – if anything, I needed to calm down.

What did I think I was doing? I'm not sure – the truth is my head was in a jumble.

I suited up in gym gear – sweatpants, an old Northwestern t-shirt, running shoes – and pocketed my NYU identification card and my iPod. As I was about to head out the door, I looked at the silver gift bag filled with possibly incriminating evidence. I thought maybe if Jimmy didn't turn up, I could use the time on the cardio machine to go over these documents. And then, at the last moment, I impulsively grabbed Kay Ambrose's little *Ballet-Lover's Pocket-Book*. As I believe I mentioned, I'd been car-rying it around with me quite a bit. I put it in with the evidence.

It was about 6 p.m. The cardio room was packed. The tread-mills were littered with the usual suspects – and I mean that in the colloquial sense. In other words, the wiry, eccentric hippie was there, along with the other familiar 40- and 50-somethings staving off impending decline, but Jimmy Stewart was nowhere to be seen. I propped my silver gift bag against the base of a StairMaster and mounted the pedals, which descended smoothly under my weight. I scrolled through "Artists" on my iPod and settled on Aldo Ciccolini playing Satie. I wanted to give this my full concentration. I programmed the StairMaster for maximized age-appropriate cardio intensity. And then I started stepping.

On the machine to my right was a woman with dyed black hair, an oversized Obama t-shirt, and bicycle shorts. She was peering down her reading glasses at the *TLS* as she chugged away. Lots of people read on these machines. I glanced down at my bag of materials, but felt somehow too overwhelmed to look at them right now. I decided to do my usual: close my eyes, step in time with the music, and just think about the problems at hand.

Ciccolini was playing *Croquis et agaceries d'un gros bonhomme en bois*. The rhythm was anxious, and I stepped accordingly. The title of the piece reminded me of that enormous sculpture of Davy Crockett. I felt the massive wooden gentleman thudding away behind me as I climbed, climbed, climbed the never-ending slope of the StairMaster. My mind zig-zagged through the hilly terrain of Phoenicia, the revving engines of the local bikers buzzing threateningly around me. I climbed, climbed up the steep incline of Mesnička Street in Zagreb, where I'd met Dan Ferguson that night at the gbar. I rang again at the unmarked door, slipped in unseen by passersby. I clambered up the echoing stairwell of Lennox Hill Hospital, which became Södersjukhuset, white, hygienic stairwells where I was joined at each landing by a familiar, sad figure: Ellen, the crone in the wheelchair, Sven. I climbed and I climbed. I was looking for the moth. I was looking for the freer of vassals.

But I opened my eyes and I saw Jimmy Stewart.

It was him, in the mirror, unmistakable: he had on that original costume, the tucked-in white shirt and the twill plaid tennis shorts. The yanked-up, pristine socks. His tiny racquet was leaning against his machine as he nimbly stepped on the pedals. He smiled at me. I felt a tingling sensation rising from my feet to the top of my head. I felt my foot slip a little across the pedal as I pitched slightly forward.

The next thing I knew, the eccentric hippie was leaning over me, propping my head up and offering me a sip from the bottle of water he'd been balancing on the top of his head. He was saying, "Just take it easy, man. Have a little water. You just gotta watch your heart rate."

The woman with the dyed hair had also dismounted and was watching me with some concern. She asked the hippie, "Do you think I should call somebody?"

I said, "No, really, I'm okay..."

She said, "Maybe it's low blood sugar. Did you eat enough today? It's not good to exercise on a totally empty stomach. I have a banana in my locker. Does anybody have some Gatorade?"

I'd fainted, of course. It wasn't my heart rate, and it wasn't low blood sugar. It was sheer terror. And then I realized: the silver gift bag was gone. So was Jimmy Stewart.

I scrambled home as quickly as I could. Jorge opened the door for me and could see something was wrong. He said, "Escuse me for asking, sir, but are you feeling okay?" I said I was just a little dizzy but I'd be fine.

When I got up to my sublet I started flipping out. I double-locked the door. I checked in the closets, the bathroom, and the balcony just to make sure nobody had snuck in while I was out. I knew I didn't have enough evidence to call the cops. I wondered if I should at least let a friend know the mess I'd gotten myself into – but whom to call? Sven couldn't do anything from Stockholm, and besides, this would just upset him. Same went for Ellen who was still staying with her mother. Randy and Jeremy were extremely nice, and might even appreciate the Hardy Boys elements of the story, but would they actually take it seriously? Dan and Fang seemed kind of young and innocent to rope into something like this. José Muñoz would surely suggest something pragmatic, like approaching the Campus Police – not an option as far as I was concerned. If Jimmy had buffaloed Galina at the Torch Club, I was sure he could hoodwink some second-rate campus security guards.

I knew I couldn't get any work done, and any further sleuthing at this point would just put me over the edge. No use trying to read or otherwise "distract" myself. I poked around the bathroom and found a bottle of NyQuil. I poured myself a dose in the little plastic cup and gulped it down. And then I poured another. I didn't have a cold, and I wasn't trying to harm myself. I just wanted to go to sleep. I brushed my teeth and lay down in my bed, hoping desperately that when I woke up, this all would have been a dream.

No such luck. I fell asleep all right, but after a fitful night of creepy dreams, I woke with the first crack of light piercing my curtains. I glanced at the clock: 6:42 a.m. I washed my face and brushed my teeth. I made some espresso in my little espresso pot. While it was bubbling, I did some stretching and then went to the door to get *The New York Times*.

Sitting there, right next to the *Times*, was my silver gift bag.

Oh. My. God.

I reached down and picked it up. Everything appeared to be intact. The manuscript was there, along with my sketchy notes, and the little book by Miss Ambrose.

But there was something else in there. An envelope.

I picked up the newspaper as well, and brought everything inside, setting it all on the coffee table. I went back into the kitchen and poured my coffee, lightening it with half and half. I took a sip to steel myself. I returned to the living room and sat on the sofa. I breathed deeply. This was the moment of truth. I reached into the gift bag.

My hands trembling slightly, I opened the envelope and

pulled out a carefully creased piece of onionskin paper, practically covered, top to bottom, edge to edge, with single-spaced, typewritten text.

My heart pounded as I read it.

Jimmy was onto me. He'd seen my notes. He knew I was writing a novel and he knew I'd been stalking him for material – him and his friends. Well, all right then. He could understand that. As an artist himself, he knew that one always walked a fine line between using people and paying tribute to them, and that in the end it was the integrity of the artwork that would take precedence over the feelings of the "little people." In this case, himself, the tiny dancer, and her pal the freshener. And while Jimmy was well aware that, for his part, certain aspects of his demeanor might lend an air of mystery or comedy to my project, he wanted to make sure, just for his own peace of mind, that I really understood where he was coming from. He knew this may not end up in my novel – it was between him and me. Man to man. One artist to another.

```
After all, murder is - or should be -
an art. Not one of the "seven lively,"
perhaps, but an art nevertheless.
   :)
   But seriously, Mr. Adams. Are you
interested in solving this case or in
making me look foolish?
   The way the evidence has piled
up against me, I can't say I blame
you much. I have no defense against
forged papers! I stand guilty as
FRAMED! But I've got a few things I
want to say. I tried to say them once
before, and I got stopped colder 'n a
mackerel. Well, I'd like to get them
```

```
said this time, sir. I've got a piece
to speak, and blow hot or cold, I'm
going to speak it.
```

He realized his collaboration with Nethermost might seem improbable. But for all their apparent differences, there were certain values they shared: above all, an appreciation of life itself. The freshener was with them on this. And in their own weird ways, all those dead genii had been, too.

Jimmy acknowledged this simplistic explanation might not win him so many points in my "egghead" set. But he wasn't making any apologies.

```
I'd like people to remember me as
someone who was good at his job and
seemed to mean what he said.
My mother used to say to me, "in
this world, you must be oh so smart,
or oh so pleasant." For years I was
smart. Yeah, that's probably the first
thing you noticed about me that you
liked - my colossal brain. I recommend
pleasant. And you may quote me.
```

Jimmy registered some skepticism regarding the Derridean analyses of the questions of love and loss in my manuscript. He directed me to check out his marginalia on page 214, where next to my footnote on Heidegger's distinction between "properly dying" (*tod-eigentlich sterben*) and "perishing" (*verenden*) he had scrawled, emphatically, "??????!!!!!!!!" My theoretical bag of tricks was just not doing it for him, and in all honesty, I'd have to say he had a point.

```
I wouldn't give you two cents for
```

```
all your fancy rules, if behind them
they didn't have a little ordinary
everyday human kindness, and a little
lookin'out for the other fella, too. I
have my own rules and adhere to them.
The rule is simple but inflexible...
it will be clean, and it will involve
the triumph of the underdog over the
bully. Well, don't knock it. That's
the American Dream. And in this
world today, full of hatred, a man
who knows that one rule has a great
trust.
    You know, everybody's afraid to
live.
    Every time I think about how lucky I
am, I feel like screaming.
```

I let that one sink in.

I wondered if he was going to make mention of "the Duke"
– and of course he did. And while the very act of typing his
handle now sends a shiver up my spine, I confess that Jimmy
Stewart's defense of him had a quiet dignity I found almost
redemptive:

```
Courageous. And decent. He was
also far from perfect. He made his
mistakes as I have made mine and you
have made yours. All in all, I would
say they were unintentional. Mistakes
of the heart, I would say.
```

Well.

The closing lines of Jimmy's letter were simultaneously so

self-knowing and so psychotic, I really didn't know what to do
with them. They were Schechnerian performance theory pushed
to its logical conclusion, which was nothing less than transcen-
dence, and utter madness:

```
I am James Stewart playing James
Stewart. I couldn't mess around
with the characterizations. I
play variations on myself. I'm the
inarticulate man who tries. I don't
really have all the answers, but for
some reason, somehow, I make it.
   Sometimes I wonder if I'm doing a
Jimmy Stewart impersonation myself.
```

What did I feel? What would *you* feel? Shame. Terror.
Recognition. Love.

Two days later, the moth posted another video.

It was clearly produced in tender collaboration with Jimmy Stewart, whom I could no longer bring myself to refer to, even to myself, as the email jerk, even if he'd made up the moniker himself. He was, in truth, the inarticulate man who tries, foraging out into the world with his undersized guitar, his miniature racquet, his outmoded attempts at gentlemanly decorum, his mistakes of the heart. She had apparently understood this before I had.

It completed the cycle of Satie's *Gnossiennes*. But this time, the instrumentation was neither classical nor psychedelic – it was creaky, homemade, and fragile. The left hand chords clinked delicately on a toy piano, while the melody was sung in a haunting, tremulous falsetto. The choreography was pantomimic in that same earnest way that her very first dance had been – but this time the narrative she told was one all too familiar to me. It was my own. She danced my anxious prowl, my fumbling investigation, my groping ascent on the StairMaster. She danced my awkward flail, my graceless clink, my humiliating fall. She danced the lines of my pedantic research, my stammering exegesis, the blurted agony of my realizations.

In her diminutive interpretation, my story suddenly made sense. It wasn't the shocking drama I had imagined. It was the pocket-sized solution to the mystery that had been dogging me for months.

Perhaps you've figured out what this story is about. It took a while for me to see it myself. It was a mystery, but it wasn't the one I thought it was.

It was the impossibly ponderous question I'd been unable to articulate myself: Why do the people we love have to die?

The answer was simple, unsatisfactory, and dumb.

Because.

It was my story she'd danced, so I knew I needed to leave a comment. But that meant I had to stop just lurking and give myself a name. I had to register on YouTube. I considered the possibilities: PansyAmidLaggards, SlangySadParadigm, MyAddlingAsparagus. SagPiddlyAnagrams. Finally I chose: PudgyGrandmasAlias. And under this byline, I left my simple response: "Thank you." I also subscribed to her channel.

AhNestermostFun promptly piped up: "I'm nobody! Who are you?"

Without waiting for me to answer, ACabFreshenerOnTypos jumped in: "What am I, after all, but a child, pleas'd with the sound of my own name? repeating it over and over: AgelessFavors, GolfAverseAss, LasersOfVegas... To you, your name also; Did you think there was nothing but two or three pronunciations in the sound of your name? LissomePenknifeDichotomy, CoifedSemimonthlyPinkoes..."

ThyMusketEmailJerk interrupted: "quit ur sqwaukin we got wrk to do. mybe we cn do gfi wth a twst. I alwys thot it needed a twst. u dnt like that. r we an indy bnd or are we lounge sngrs?"

They were obviously off on a roll, discussing the next collaboration. I backed off and waited to see what would happen.

The Girl from Ipanema

*I*t appeared three months later.

Why so long? It was something of a grand finale, and it looked like it had required the coordination of a number of individuals. Everybody turned up in the moth's bathtub, one by one: the moth herself, of course, coyly swiveling her hips around the basin; that skinny adolescent (he got a hair cut!), poking his long fingers at a toy piano; the delicate older gentleman dancing with his eyes closed... Jimi Hendrix showed up! Decked out in suede, he shredded while leaning into the tiled corner of the tub. The mysterious falsetto hid behind the frosted glass of the shower enclosure. But another singer displayed herself plainly: it was that handsome woman from the *pas de deux*. "You'll know Her – by Her Voice." She was a mezzo-soprano! That was a surprise.

Yet the greatest revelation was this: as the unmistakable, orgasmically beautiful howl of the cab freshener's electric guitar emerged, the camera revealed her identity: a woman, small, roughly the moth's size, though muscular, manhandling her axe with an authoritative sexuality, her peroxided hair splaying energetically around her concentrated face. Her bassist, too, flung her locks sidewise as she explored the deepest groove of "The Girl from Ipanema."

The freer of vassals is, was, had always been – female.

The last to appear was Jimmy Stewart. Quiet, dignified, he solemnly fingerpicked his baritone uke, finding a narrow opening in that cacophony to add his simple accompaniment. And as the melody faded away, he looked up at the camera. It was a look of total candor.

He was one more freak in the odd assemblage of that bathtub extravaganza. One more American minimalist who had his own rules and adhered to them. He never wanted to hurt the moth. They were two peas in a pod, babe. Two peas in a pod.

Jimmy Stewart was the moth's dear friend, along with all the others. The toy pianist was her son. The freer of vassals was her lesbian lover.

They were family.

What, you may wonder, had been happening in the other realms of my life during their artistic hiatus? Well, with the onset of the spring semester, things had started to pick up again at

NYU. Steve Kurtz came, and I attended a public lecture he gave with Fang. He was extremely intelligent without being intimidating. He recounted an interventionist project he'd staged with some Canadian students. Being Canadian, they wanted to apologize as a form of political activism. Apparently he helped them to mount a lot of apologetic messages in public places, and once again he was suspected of "terrorism," but when he explained things to the Canadian police, they were also apologetic.

Fang initiated the filiform wart performance but fortunately it didn't take. I didn't tell her I thought it was all for the best, but Steve Kurtz did. She started a new project measuring trace amounts of residual sexual fluids on US paper currency.

In February I gave Bugs Bunny's sister a small heart-shaped box of Russell Stover chocolates for Valentine's Day. She seemed to like this.

Sven and I exchanged texts saying, "<3."

Ellen came back from her mother's at the beginning of March. She was a little plumper and it suited her.

There was another little glitch with the rent check that month, but I managed to straighten things out.

The Dean of the Faculty of the Arts at the University of Malta wrote to request an interview with me via Skype. We scheduled it for April 1st. I realized that was April Fool's Day.

Randy and Jeremy had a party at their place in Manhattan and I went with Ellen. It was Jeremy's birthday (Pisces – coincidentally, he shared his birthday with Ruth Bader Ginsburg). I made pralines. I spent most of the evening speaking with their neighbor, who was some kind of Latvian aristocrat and very, very old. Jeremy told me she stood out in front of the building and had one cigarette every evening, no matter how cold or rainy it might be. I think he said she was 93. She used to live in Buenos Aires.

Richard Schechner wrote to tell me that my paper had been accepted for publication in *TDR*. That was the good news. The bad news was I received another e-mail from Ramon Gonzalez asking me for a title for my spring semester presentation. It was scheduled for May 4.

I had made zero progress on the revisions to my academic manuscript. Still, instead of giving him one more time that ungainly title of my dissertation, I gave him the revised title I'd made up for the more "accessible" version I'd imagined I'd have finished by now.

At the end of March, Dan, Fang, and I attended a lecture at the department by Neal Medlyn, "the Paris Hilton of performance art." Neal Medlyn is the author of the book *Sexual Buttocks* and also *Ars Nova*, an opera based on the works of Lionel Ritchie. This was going to be a tough act to follow.

My Skype interview seemed to go fairly smoothly.

Sven arrived April 5. On April 6 I took him to a public event honoring Mario Montez, the Warhol superstar who got his start with Jack Smith. Mario was in full drag and looked really beautiful. He sipped his water through a straw, evidently in order to avoid messing up his lipstick. He was without irony and completely straightforward in discussing his career as an actor. We were very moved.

That week we watched *Unfaithfully Yours* by Preston Sturges. In the film, a snooty orchestra conductor (Rex Harrison) thinks his wife is having an affair. He fantasizes three different responses to the situation while conducting three different Romantic-era compositions. To Rossini, he imagines killing his wife and framing her lover for the murder. To Wagner, he imagines himself generously sending her off with her new lover and a big fat check. And to Tchaikovsky, he imagines bravely playing a game of Russian roulette with his blubbering rival (in this version, it's unfortunately Rex Harrison who blows his brains out). I'd have to say it's not often I consider myself "Wagnerian," but in this case, I did. Of course it turns out the wife wasn't having an affair at all. Sven found the movie a little hokey.

He seemed to be feeling a little less vulnerable these days.

He'd decided to try the FOTO regimen. His numbers were still excellent, and his stomach problems were starting to diminish.

:)

I looked on the Air Malta website and noticed that there was a very convenient and reasonably priced direct flight between Stockholm and Luqa.

I avoided thinking about my income taxes until April 15 and at the eleventh hour used some tax return software I downloaded. Believe it or not, despite my abject circumstances, I owed the IRS money. I requested a deferred payment plan.

The weather was improving. On nice days, Bugs Bunny's sister again took to sunning herself just outside the entrance to our building.

The last week in April, I sat in front of my computer wondering what the hell I was going to say in my final presentation in the department.

I also did a lot of *barre* exercises and stared across the court-yard at the balcony with the stationary bicycle. I hadn't returned to the cardio room at the gym since my humiliating collapse.

On May 1 – May Day – I received an e-mail alert from YouTube that AhNethermostFun had posted a new video. My heart leapt when I read this. I hesitated, and clicked on the link.

That was it: the grand finale, the collaborative *tour de force*, "The Girl from Ipanema."

If her penultimate choreography had mimed back to me my own flailing life, this one appeared to be a careful, meticulous explanation of hers. It was an aggregation of unassuming virtuosi, lo-res, lo-fi, captured in miniature – the singular, extraordinary "little people" that revolved through her tiny world.

May 4, if you'll excuse the expression, I pulled it out my ass again. Once more, my talk was providentially scheduled at the exhausted, slap-happy end of the semester, just before a final bash. Ramon made sure the YouTube connection was set up and the projector was functioning. This time Lepecki graciously recited my bona fides.

I stepped up to the lectern and said, "A woman in a black leotard, her dark hair pulled back, is dancing a subdued dance in an interior space – her living room? There are some peculiar paintings on the wall." I clicked on the YouTube link.

I read directly from the manuscript of my novel.

A few days later, I got a call from the Dean at the University of Malta offering me the position. I decided to take it. It came in the nick of time, as my fellowship was just running out.

I called my mother and told her I wanted to come and visit her in Wisconsin before I moved to Malta in July. That seemed to make her happy. Sven and I talked about what the move would mean for our relationship. It seemed like we'd probably continue our schedule of visits, but he'd be visiting me in Msida instead of New York. We'd see how that worked out.

When they found out about my job, Dan and Fang wanted to take me out to celebrate, but we decided to do it at the PSi conference in Toronto. We'd all booked cheapo rooms in a dormitory at Ryerson University. It resembled a cellblock. On the first night of the conference, we met in front of the dormitory and walked over to Tallulah's Cabaret for the opening performance event.

Several of Canada's premiere performance artists and ensembles were on the bill. The best one was Jess Dobkin. She came out onto the stage dressed like Kermit the Frog. Actually, she wasn't really dressed. She was naked, but painted green from head to toe, with the exception of her pubic hair. She began limply slumping on a stool. Then a jaunty, strapping woman entered, dressed like Jim Henson. She had a bushy beard. She slipped her right hand into a rubber glove, and proceeded to insert the whole thing into Dobkin's vagina. This appeared to animate Kermit, who then lip-synced "It's Not Easy Being Green" as though she were in fact a puppet being manipulated by Jim Henson. It was virtuosic, no doubt about it. I heard José Muñoz saying afterwards, "I'm not usually a big one for naked, but I must say, that was pretty impressive."

After the performance, Dan and Fang and I went to a nearby bar and ordered beer and poutine, which was gross, but seemed like the thing to do at the time. I said, "Who knew that Canadian performance art could be so *outré*?" Dan said that Jess Dobkin was originally from the U.S. but that the Canadians had accepted her with open arms.

It's not easy being green in America. It's also not easy being black, or brown, or gay, or a woman, or a man. It's not easy being old, anywhere.

It's not easy loving somebody, and it's not easy being alone. It's not easy being strapped for cash and it's not easy being an artist. None of this is for sissies. Even in Sweden. Even in Canada.

I don't think I've ever described myself as a "greedy man," but I guess I am. I know all the pitfalls, but if I'm going to be honest, I'd have to say that life's been good to me, and I want some more of it.

Who knows what Malta will bring.

ACKNOWLEDGMENTS

All YouTube comments attributed to falserebelmoth / AhNethermostFun were cribbed, as the astute reader will have surmised without recourse to Google, from the poetry of Emily Dickinson. Similarly, all comments by GoFreeVassals / ACabFreshenerOnTypos can be traced to Walt Whitman.

The contents of Jimmy Stewart's typewritten missive to Gray have all been attributed to the "real" Jimmy Stewart, or characters played by him, on a variety of questionable Internet sites. The same goes for statements posted by "the Duke." Most but not all of the other weird, touching, horrifying and baffling YouTube comments are attributed to their original sources.

The author shamelessly availed herself of www.wordsmith.org in constructing her characters' anagrammatic monikers and couldn't fault readers for availing themselves of the site in order to retrace her steps. There are surely better and worse ways to waste time pondering one's difficulties in dealing with intimacy, identity, aging and mortality.

The following individuals supplied talent, inspiration, help, encouragement, cautionary advice, and/or editorial comments, but are not to be held responsible for anything: Mr. Otis Chutney, Yen Fum (Chicano), Viola Lei Roe, Fay Streamer, Divine Concavi, Dim

Heckled Tart, Infidel Smoker, Abner
Morfitt, Caramel Jetsam, Nice Doc Dinion,
Ms. Rena Cage Vivaldi, Tactician Pearl
Roma, El Freaky Nin, Banana Ott (muse),
Mojo Zenus, Jaws Hornden, Comrade Noritz,
General Nil Nip, Seaman Kirk Whaa, Amelia
Crud, Gala Dingus, Calipered Ken, Omar
F. Krank, Nelly DeMan, Igor Welchino,
Herr Chris Drench (cad), Vanity A. Goon,
Viz Sarah Salt, Yo Dun Yang, Rajah Tam
Nonevent, Berry Valet, Octaveo Sloane,
DJ Ben Sisko, Lee Roi (waitress), Nosy
Chevalier, Alabaster Curlicue Gem, Bethel
O. (Kamikaze), Faerie Bunco, Woeful Booze
Naiad, Lumpy Nellie, Lil' Ms. Nubile Peak,
Oily Krebs Zitwit, Vito Mashken, Wiltsy
O'Kibitzer, Aha Thin Bean, Sir Anatomist
Fessing, Twigs Dunno, Cloud Nine (CIA),
Jeer Yam Hymn, Keen Eons, Golly Mis Eel,
Rich Sward, Auxin Teed Blowhard, and, of
course, Ultimo Mall Wino. I spent a whole
day doing that.

THE ORANGE EATS CREEPS
A NOVEL BY GRACE KRILANOVICH
A Trade Paperback Original; 978-0-9820151-8-6; $16 US
  * National Book Foundation 2010 '5 Under 35' Selection.
  * *NPR* Best Books of 2010.
  * *The Believer* Book Award Finalist.
  * Amazon's Top Ten Science Fiction/Fantasy Books of 2010

"Krilanovich's work will make you believe that new ways of storytelling are still emerging from the margins." —*NPR*

THE CORRESPONDENCE ARTIST
A NOVEL BY BARBARA BROWNING
A Trade Paperback Original; 978-0-9820151-9-3; $16 US
  * Finalist for a 2012 Lambda Literary Award.

"A deft look at modern life that's both witty and devastating."
—*Nylon*

"Intelligent... a pleasure to read." —*Bookslut*

THE CAVE MAN
A NOVEL BY XIAODA XIAO
A Trade Paperback Original; 978-0-9820151-3-1; $15.50 US
  * *WOSU* (NPR member station) Favorite Book of 2009.
"As a parable of modern China, [*The Cave Man*] is chilling."
—*Boston Globe*

THE VISITING SUIT
A NOVEL BY XIAODA XIAO
A Trade Paperback Original; 978-0-9820151-7-9; $16.50 US
"[Xiao] recount[s] his struggle in sometimes unexpectedly lovely detail. Against great odds, in the grimmest of settings, he manages to find good in the darkness."
—Lori Soderlind, *New York Times Book Review*

SEVEN DAYS IN RIO
A NOVEL BY FRANCIS LEVY
A Trade Paperback Original; 978-0-9826848-7-0; $16.00 US

"The funniest American novel since Sam Lipsyte's *The Ask*."
—*Village Voice*

"Like an erotic version of Luis Bunuel's *The Discreet Charm of the Bourgeoisie*." —*The Cult*

THE PEOPLE WHO WATCHED HER PASS BY
A NOVEL BY SCOTT BRADFIELD
A Trade Paperback Original; 978-0-9820151-5-5; $14.50 US

"Challenging [and] original... A billowy adventure of a book. In a book that supplies few answers, Bradfield's lavish eloquence is the presiding constant."
—*New York Times Book Review*

THE DROP EDGE OF YONDER
A NOVEL BY RUDOLPH WURLITZER
A Trade Paperback Original; 978-0-9763895-5-2; $15.00 US
   * *Time Out New York*'s Best Book of 2008.
   * *ForeWord* Magazine 2008 Gold Medal in Literary Fiction.
"A picaresque American *Book of the Dead*... in the tradition of Thomas Pynchon, Joseph Heller, Kurt Vonnegut, and Terry Southern." —*Los Angeles Times*

BABY GEISHA
STORIES BY TRINIE DALTON
A Trade Paperback Original; 978-0-9832471-0-4; $16 US

"[The stories] feel like brilliant sexual fairy tales on drugs. Dalton writes of self-discovery and sex with a knowing humility and humor."
—*Interview Magazine*